Race for the Park Street Treasure

Accidental Detectives Mysteries

Race for the Park Street Treasure

SIGMUND BROUWER

VICTOR BOOKS

A DIVISION OF SCRIPTURE PRESS PUBLICATIONS INC.
USA CANADA ENGLAND

THE ACCIDENTAL DETECTIVES SERIES

Lost Beneath Manhattan
The Mystery Tribe of Camp Blackeagle
Phantom Outlaw at Wolf Creek
The Disappearing Jewel of Madagascar
The Missing Map of Pirate's Haven
Creature of the Mists

Race for the Park Street Treasure
The Downtown Desperadoes
Madness at Moonshiner's Bay
Sunrise at the Mayan Temple
Short Cuts
Terror on Kamikaze Run

Cover illustration by Suzanne Garnier
Photo and illustrations by Dwight Arthur

Library of Congress Cataloging-in-Publication Data

Brouwer, Sigmund, 1959-
　　Race for the Park Street treasure / by Sigmund W. Brouwer.
　　　　p.　　cm. — (The Accidental detectives)
　　Summary: As Ricky and his friends search for a treasure buried long
ago by a tightwad business tycoon, Ricky sees how ugly — and danger-
ous — the depths of greed can become.
　　ISBN 1-56476-376-5
　　[1. Mystery and detective stories. 2. Buried treasure — Fiction.
3. Christian life — Fiction.] I. Title. II. Series: Brouwer, Sigmund, 1959-
Accidental detectives.
PZ7.B79984Rac 1991
　　[Fic] — dc20　　　　　　　　　　　　　　　　　　　　91-18971
　　　　　　　　　　　　　　　　　　　　　　　　　　　　CIP
　　　　　　　　　　　　　　　　　　　　　　　　　　　　AC

　　　　4　　5　　6　　7　　8　　9　　10　　Printing/Year　　99　　98　　97　　96　　95

VICTOR BOOKS
A division of SP Publications, Inc.
Wheaton, Illinois 60187

To Pat and Stephanie Lawrence —
thank you for being friends.

Nobody hangs around Mike Andrews when he's itching to displace good energy into a bad idea. At least, nobody smart.

Unfortunately, I wasn't thinking.

It was a Saturday morning in the middle of September. We had been back in school less than two weeks and already it seemed my brains were permanently stuck in the middle row, surrounded by math equations and history dates.

That was my excuse. Plus the fact that it *was* Saturday morning, the day of the week that makes you want to bust for action at the best of times. Worse for Mike's itch, it was a perfect Saturday. The sky was dusty blue as far as I could see, the air as crisp as the blazing leaves which filled the huge oak tree in Mike's backyard.

A great day in our small town of Jamesville for football. Or street hockey. Or stopping by Old Man Jacobsen's to accidentally shake loose the apples which would fall anyway with or without our help. A great day for anything but taking Mike Andrews' advice.

I said as much.

He grinned back, the grin that has earned more chocolate chip cookies from more grumpy old ladies than should be possible.

"Football? Street hockey? With who?" He swept his arms in all directions. "All I see are you, me, and Ralphy."

Ralphy—computer genius and bundle of nerves—hung his head and smiled shyly.

"Unless Joel's nearby," I replied. Joel was my ghostlike six-year-old brother. Mike looked around nervously. He too had a healthy fear of my brother's terrifying powers.

"Joel or no Joel, Ricky, my point is this," Mike said. "We need more players than just the three of us."

"All we need is one more," I said stubbornly. "Four gives us enough for street hockey."

"Sure." Mike's grin became almost devilish. "Lisa Higgins?"

Lisa Higgins is as much trouble as Joel. The difference is that Joel remains largely unseen, while Lisa you notice immediately.

She's twelve, like the rest of us, and doesn't have to be a tiny ghost like Joel to drive us nuts. The first area of concern is her prettiness. It breaks through once in a while when you're trying to treat her like a pal and makes you cough or stutter until you remember again she's only a girl. Long dark hair and eyes like a perfect September sky. When she smiles, it's a beam of sunshine breaking through dark clouds; when she's mad, all you see are the dark clouds.

Worse, she's good at sports, which is what Mike was waiting for me to admit. What she can't do, she'll practice until she's perfect. Once, Mike teased her about throwing like a girl. She spent two months every day after school pitching a baseball into the playground backstop until she could wing it so hard that the next time Mike caught one from her it sprained two of his fingers.

I smiled sweetly back at him. "Good idea, Mike. Lisa for street hockey. We'll give her a call."

His grin wavered.

I let him off the hook. "Ooops. She's not home," I said as I snapped my fingers. Lisa's dad was a lawyer and deputy mayor. "She's with her dad at the library for some stupid public ceremony. Too bad."

"Too bad," Mike agreed quickly. "Now about this target practice idea of mine . . . "

I shuddered. Then sighed. "Fire away."

"Good one," Ralphy giggled. "Get it, Mike? Fire away. Target practice? Fire away?"

Mike didn't hear him. He was lost in thought—unusual for him and not a good sign. Mike knelt on the grass and squinted in a line towards the car garage that hugged the corner of the backyard.

I sighed again. Maybe it *would* be worthwhile convincing Lisa to leave the library to make us look bad in street hockey.

Mike stood again and tilted that crooked grin as he surveyed us in mismatched hightop sneakers, torn jeans, and a Hawaiian shirt bright enough to burn your eyes. That was Mike Andrews. Freckles, red hair, a perpetual New York Yankees baseball cap, and a low tolerance for boredom. It made a dangerous combination.

"This should be no problem," he said. "My mom's gone for the day. We can easily hose off the garage before she gets back."

"Hose off the garage?" Ralphy's voice did not carry a trace of its previous giggle. If something in his life is not as regular as the sun rising, it makes him nervous.

"Yes. Hose off the garage. You think we want to leave watermelon on it forever?"

"Watermelon?" This time Ralphy's voice quivered.

"Yes. Watermelon. Are you going to repeat everything I say?"

"Repeat everything—?"

"Forget I asked." Mike began trotting toward the garage. "I'll be right back with a wheelbarrow."

"Don't say it," I warned Ralphy as Mike creaked the door open and stepped out of our sight.

He did anyway. "Wheelbarrow?"

Mike returned almost immediately with, yes, a wheelbarrow. A huge, old-fashioned wheelbarrow with long, thick wooden handles. He moved it to the corner of the yard farthest from the garage. Without speaking, he spun around and went back, then emerged with a shovel.

He waved us over. We joined him reluctantly. We were as far away from the garage as possible without leaving the yard. The bushes along the fence poked our backsides.

"This is the deal," Mike said as he handed me the shovel. "We need a hole. Be careful with this top layer of sod. We'll need to put it back in place when we're finished."

I held the shovel away from me and lifted one eyebrow in his direction. "I do enough yard work at home," I said.

"You *have* to dig. I'm the one going into the grocery store garbage bin to find the rotting watermelons they throw away."

"Sure, Mike. I'll be happy to dig. Right down to China," I said. "But whatever you do, don't tell me why. Or even how big the hole should be."

My sarcasm bounced off his pumpkin-sized grin. "Ralphy will explain. I'll be back in a flash."

He hitched his jeans before going, then stopped to grab his skateboard from the back porch and hit the ground running.

"Ralphy Zee," I began threateningly. "You *did* know about the wheelbarrow."

"Not everything," he protested.

Ralphy responds quite well to threats. He's skinny with straight hair that points in all directions. A wrinkled, too-large shirt always hangs out the back of his pants or gets caught in fences whenever we take shortcuts. The only time he isn't nervous is in front of a computer. There he becomes graceful and confident and serene—a swan on water. Anywhere else, and he's an awkward duck on land.

"I didn't think he'd take it seriously," he rushed on as I continued my glare. "I was just talking experimental physics. How was I to know he'd really want to try it out against a garage."

I groaned. "Experimental physics. Spill the rest, pal."

He did. By the time he finished, I was grinning. It wasn't such a bad idea. And, best of all, it was Mike's garage. There was no way I could get into trouble on this one.

When Mike rejoined us, carrying two potato sacks bulging with watermelons, Ralphy and I were nearly ready.

There was a hole in the ground deep enough and wide enough to bury most of the wheelbarrow. We tilted it upright and slid it down. All that stuck out of the ground were the two thick wooden handles, each one pointing straight at the sky.

Lost in his world of scientific experiments, Ralphy became a general. "OK, guys. Dump dirt back into the hole and pack it so that the wheelbarrow becomes steady as a rock."

While Mike and I diligently packed earth against the submerged wheelbarrow, Ralphy zipped to the garage and struggled back with an old tractor tire tube that was bigger than he was.

Mike looked at me. "I know, I know. But we'll replace it before next summer. It's not as if we can do any river rafting until then anyway."

I shrugged. At this point, I was all for experimental physics.

Ralphy ignored us. He pulled a jackknife from his pocket — razor sharp, of course, because Ralphy is a perfectionist — and began slashing the wide rubber of the tire tube.

While he did that, Mike wandered over to the garage and tacked a cardboard target onto the side wall.

As they worked, I could hear the far-off sounds of somebody using a squeaky microphone. *Hah*, I thought, *Lisa Higgins is stuck listening to a boring speech, and we're having fun with experiments.*

Ralphy dug into his pockets and found some lengths of thick string.

"Now comes the tricky part." He stuck the ends of the string in his mouth to keep his hands free. "Making sure these rubber bands stay attached to the handles."

Rubber bands? Sure, and roaring lions were only house cats. Ralphy was working with a wide strip of tire tube long as a car.

It took him another five or ten minutes, long enough for some parade music to drift our way. I thought of Lisa and gloated silently again. *If she only knew the fun we were having.*

Ralphy finished and stepped back to survey his work.

"Experimental physics at its best," Mike announced.

Two solid wood handles stuck out of the ground. One end of the huge rubber band was secured to one handle, the other end to the second handle. The long loop of the rubber between rested limply on the ground. Waiting for action.

Ralphy beamed and admired. I grinned inside. The three of us were looking at the world's largest slingshot.

Mike broke our respectful moment of awe.

"Target practice time," he said.

I had a terrible thought. "Is the garage strong enough to take the impact?"

"Of course," he said in an impatient tone. "These are rotten watermelons, nice and soft."

Ralphy agreed. "In fact," he said, "these watermelons are so rotten, we'll have to make sure to hold only the rubber itself as we pull back."

I ignored my misgivings about the strength of the garage wall and nodded.

Mike carefully loaded the watermelon into the loop of rubber. "Ralphy, keep it in place while Ricky and I stretch this baby to full power."

I understood immediately why we couldn't hold the watermelon as we backed up. The strain of bracing it against the rubber band would have crushed it within seconds.

"Far enough?" I grunted.

"Nope." Mike's eyes were bulging from the effort it took to hold the rubber. "I want to *fire* this baby. We can stretch this another two feet."

We almost did.

One foot farther back—it took five more seconds of sheer leg power to get there—my brother and his teddy bear appeared like smoke from the bushes along the fence.

"I'll help," he announced.

"Uggh . . . no," I managed to say against the effort it took to keep my grip.

Joel ignored me and studied our efforts. "Better let me push," he said. He set his teddy bear down carefully, and walked around the wheelbarrow handles, then through them and straight toward us. *Dead center in our sights.*

"Don't . . . let . . . go . . . " I pleaded to Mike between gritted teeth.

Joel did not see the danger in helping out his big brother. He marched up to the watermelon and placed his two little hands against it.

"I'm pushing now," he said with solemn eyes. "How far?"

"Move," I hissed.

Joel gritted his teeth with stubbornness. "I'm going to help."

"No."

"Yes."

It's useless to try changing his mind when his jaw is set like that.

My arms were screaming in fatigue. I couldn't hold much longer. Yet, if Mike or I so much as slipped one ounce in strength, Joel would be as much of a cannonball as the watermelon. *What to do?*

Then I remembered! "Ralphy . . . get . . . your . . . knife . . . and . . . cut . . . the . . . band."

It was our only way out. As soon as his knife sliced through the rubber, the slingshot would lose all power. Joel would be safe.

Wrong.

What happened next went in terrible slow motion that I replayed again and again for the rest of the day.

Ralphy stepped back from holding the watermelon in place. The rubber was so tight at that point, that the watermelon did not drop. Ralphy pulled his knife out of his pocket and Joel — Mr. Attention Span himself — decided getting a closer look at it was more important than helping us push. He ducked and came up on our side.

My nerves were as tight as the rubber band and Joel's sudden movement was enough to startle me into relaxing my grip for a split second. That in turn put the total strain on Mike and he yelped. His yelp made me jump and I let go just as Mike's feet slipped. With a gigantic snap we lost our tug-of-war against our slingshot band.

The watermelon did not hit the target which Mike had so carefully pinned into place. It did not hit the side of the garage. Nor the roof of the garage. In fact, the watermelon did not come remotely close as it soared into the dusty blue sky and out of our sight. "Oh, nuts," I said.

We all held our breaths in dread. Would it be a crashing of glass? Cars screeching to a stop? How much trouble had we just bought ourselves?

The seconds seemed like hours, and in our concentrated horror of waiting for the impending sound of doom, the drifting parade music a block over seemed like the background of a scary movie.

Then it came, the dreaded impact as that watermelon bomb finally whomped down to earth. Its heavy and loud thump reached us just as clearly as did the terrified bleat of a tuba alone in a parade of sudden silence.

Mike bit his knuckle thoughtfully. "We'd better get our bikes," he said. "With the wind behind us and no flat tires, we could be 50, maybe 60, miles from here by dark."

It could have been worse. Lots worse.

Lisa told me later that the watermelon whistled within two feet of fat Mayor Thorpe, Deputy Mayor Higgins, and Old Lady Bugsby in her starched black dress as the three of them fought over the microphone on the temporary stage which was directly beside the statue that got knocked over instead.

But it could have been better. Lots better.

The statue had not been built for the impact of a ten-pound watermelon moving too fast to be seen. So it broke into three pieces. The top piece toppled onto the stage before crashing to the ground, and the other, lower two parts of the statue shot into the front row of the parade band.

The trumpets and clarinets in the front row had not been built to be dropped and run over by a stampede of distressed musicians.

And none of the old people there to pay their respects to the statue of Old Lady Bugsby's father had been built for the excitement of thousands of bits of exploding watermelon and a suddenly hysterical wave of high school band members.

After seriously considering Mike's idea to leave town permanently, we'd slowly walked to our impending doom. We had our first inkling of the disaster when Mrs. McKinnley—who is usual-

ly slower than her puffy cats—waddled past us without the help
of the cane she uses to swat kids slow enough to stay within
range. Right behind her was Mr. McKinnley, stumping along and
croaking for someone to call the President because the Germans
had just attacked.

"Ricky," Mike said as he stopped to stare at the two of them
disappearing down the street, "it's still not too late to run away."

"Maybe Australia," Ralphy added wistfully. "I read somewhere
about ships that let you work on board to pay for your ticket."

"How bad can it be?" I argued. "You don't hear an ambulance,
do you? If nobody got hurt, no one can be too mad at us. Right?"

Wrong. Wrong. Wrong. Even in the confusion around the fallen
statue, it only took thirty seconds after our arrival for Old Lady
Bugsby to notice us.

She stepped onto the remaining portion of the stage and
clutched the microphone.

"You!" she shrilled as she shook a bony finger in our direction. All eyes swiveled upon us. "Mike Andrews! Ricky Kidd!
Ralphy Zee! Whatever happened, I know it was you! And you'll
pay for what you did to my father!"

She didn't finish. Her wide-brimmed hat, as black as her
dress, fell onto her nose and choked off her next words.

Mike and Ralphy and I stared at what we had done to her
father.

Fred Bugsby, or at least his statue, was supposed to have
become a dignified addition to the front lawn of the town library.
He was one of the town's founders and so rich and cheap that
his nickname of Moth-Wallet Bugsby survived long after he did.
People figured that if he ever opened his wallet moths would fly
out. There was still a town legend that he had turned his entire
fortune into gold before burying it, simply out of spite to keep
anyone else from ever using it after he died.

Old Lady Bugsby managed to pin her hair back into a tight

bun and straighten her hat. She found her voice and shrilled into the microphone again. "I paid a small fortune for that statue! Just wait until I speak to your parents!"

We stood helpless, the guilt written all over our faces.

Mayor Thorpe, protruding red nose and big belly poking out the vest of his pin-striped suit, stepped along a widening path through the crowd as he advanced toward us.

"Is it true?" he asked quietly when he arrived. Watermelon juice and seeds still dribbled down the curve of his belly. "Whatever happened here, are you the ones responsible?"

We nodded.

"I'm afraid I'll have to take you away," he said just as quietly.

"Lock them up forever!" Old Lady Bugsby screamed at Mayor Thorpe's back as if she had heard him.

"To jail?" Ralphy's face was whiter than his faded T-shirt.

"No, not to jail, Ralphy. Away from Old Lady—I mean away from Ethel Bugsby. She's rather upset right now, and having you around won't do any good."

"We'll pay for the statue, sir." I gulped at my words.

Mayor Thorpe dropped his voice even lower. "It will cost less than you think. I think she's mostly upset because we all can see she's as tight with money as was old Moth—I mean Fred—Bugsby himself."

"Sir?"

He snorted. "The statue. Hollow and some sort of cheap metal. That's why it broke so easily. She wouldn't pay the extra expense for one made of solid bronze."

He took my arm and led us away from the disaster scene.

"So tell me," he said as a perplexed crease shifted along his wide forehead. "What was it you did this time, Mike? That ole watermelon came from out of nowhere."

Mike tried a weak grin. "Would you believe Ricky's brother got in the way of a physics experiment?"

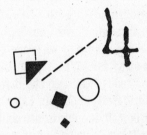

That's the trouble with a brother like Joel. Nobody ever thinks he's to blame.

I know better. But try explaining to parents that the watermelon would have been perfectly on target without interference from a six-year-old ghost. It doesn't work. They insist on asking grown-up questions like why bother with that kind of experiment in the first place.

You'd also think I would be used to Joel by now. I'm not.

No matter how many times he appears from nowhere—usually when I'm doing something that needs strict isolation—I have a heart attack and nearly jump right out of my skin. By the time I land, he's either staring at me with accusing eyes, or he'll have disappeared again just as quietly as he arrived. Joel's a terrible mixture of conscience and ghost, capable of moving like a puff of smoke.

Unfortunately, he follows me around Jamesville because he likes me. That's one reason it's hard to stay mad. The other is that he has no idea of the mess he causes by startling people with his silent and sudden appearances and disappearances.

If he didn't have his teddy bear as a weakness, he'd be invincible. The teddy bear is a battered brown and white. It has a black button for one eye and a white button for the opposite eye, but you never know which to expect because they're always falling off and getting resewn onto one side or the other.

Joel could sleep through an earthquake, but wiggle one paw of the teddy bear and his eyes pop wide open. Without that weakness, I'd never get away from him. One tactic I save for emergencies is to throw his teddy bear into the dryer. Joel patiently sits and watches until the cycle ends. But I don't overuse that tactic. Someday Joel will be tall enough to see and figure out the stop button. Also, Mom tends to notice when teddy bear button eyes fall off inside the dryer. Which always leads her to ask for the emergency reason behind my escape.

Despite that, a week later, I still regretted not using the emergency route of the dryer to keep Joel away from our giant slingshot. Because it was exactly a week later to the hour that I started my community services program. At the library.

Community service is a grown-up term for volunteer work that demonstrates honest regret for breaking a statue. We each had ten hours ahead of us—Ralphy had Old Lady Bugsby's fence to paint, Mike had the basement floor of City Hall to scrub and wax, and I had general cleanup at the town library.

As I approached the front steps of the library, I paused to wonder how something could turn out so bad and yet show no traces of disaster a week later. The stage had been hauled away. Not a single piece of statue marred the smooth, leaf-raked lawn that spread from the library's doors.

I sighed. The library was a one-story brick building, with bay windows that overlooked the park between it and City Hall. It suggested such serene quietness that I could not believe there had ever been a stampeding high school band or a brief rainstorm of watermelon.

I sighed again. *Believe it, Ricky Kidd,* I told myself. *That's why you're here.*

I trudged up the steps.

Mrs. Reynolds smiled at me from behind the checkout counter as I opened the doors.

"Well, if it isn't the Bugsby Bomber!"

"Good one, ma'am."

"We've come to expect pigeon droppings on our town statues," she grinned, "but not watermelons."

Just in case it was one of those things that stunt your growth, I fought the urge to sigh yet again. Obviously Mrs. Reynolds thought this was a joke.

I should have expected it. Ever since being Joel's age, I could remember her as a cheerful, patient librarian who encouraged me to read as often as possible. She had brown, straight hair with wisps of gray, and tended to wear longish dresses with flower patterns. She never seemed to get upset at loud whispering in the library, which happened whenever Mike followed me inside, but sure got mad if you didn't treat the books with respect.

"Um, Mrs. Reynolds? I don't really feel like talking about it. I'm not too happy about what happened."

"Nonsense. Did anyone get hurt?"

"Ralphy."

"Ralphy?"

"Yes, ma'am. I only had a long discussion with my mom and dad about responsibility. Ralphy's parents gave him a good lecture."

She tried to hide a smile. "I mean who got hurt by the watermelon?"

"Nobody."

"And didn't insurance cover the cost of the trumpets and clarinets that got trampled?"

I nodded.

"And didn't town council agree to pay for a new statue?"

I nodded again. Lisa's father—the deputy mayor—told us

later that Mayor Thorpe insisted the council vote in favor of covering the damages. Something about the best entertainment they'd had in a long time.

Mrs. Reynolds leaned forward on the checkout counter. "In other words, no permanent damage anywhere."

As I nodded agreement again, her face became serious. "Don't for a moment try to carry guilt around on this," she said. "Or on anything else. Understand? If you don't make mistakes, you're not putting any effort in living. The crime occurs when you don't learn from mistakes."

I thought about it, and as a new thought hit me, smiled back as broadly as I could. "Does this mean I won't have to work my promised ten hours?"

She came around the counter, heels clicking on the shiny floor. "Not for a second, bucko. I've got some old books in the basement which are badly in need of sorting."

I followed her to the back stairs.

Even before she found a light that showed how tiny the basement was, it seemed cramped.

It was so old that it did not have light switches. Instead, she pulled on a cord to click on a bare and dangling light bulb.

It took a few sneezes to get used to the air, and another sneeze for my eyes to adjust to the dimness away from the glare of the single light.

Support beams showed plainly against rough wood walls. The floor was simply a layer of cracked concrete.

"Nobody gets down here too often," Mrs. Reynolds noted.

I sneezed agreement.

She pointed at three boxes in the far corner. "All you have to do is this one job. Go through the old books and make two piles. One for possibly usable. One for possibly unusable. The usable pile gets priced at four for a dollar. The unusable, ten for a dollar."

"I get it. A book sale."

"Yup. So dust them carefully, and leave the stacks in alphabetical order."

"That's it?" I asked.

Mike had hours and hours of scrubbing and waxing. Ralphy had the same amount of backbreaking work on Old Lady Bugsby's fence, and all I had was some book sorting. *Hah!*

"That's it," she said absently as she moved slowly in the dim light. "Except there's a little bonus for you. You can have five books to keep as a payment for your work today." She stumbled slightly. "Oh, here's what I wanted."

She clicked on another dangling, bare bulb.

"The rest of the old books."

Wonderful.

I nearly staggered at the sight of a mountain of books and boxes against the entire wall.

"Let's see here," I muttered at the next book after at least four hours alone in the half darkness. *"A Farewell to Arms* by Ernest Hemingway. Heh. Heh. *A Farewell to Arms.* Who took the arms away, I wonder. Were they chopped off, or pulled off? Instead of saying farewell to them, I'd look for a doctor. Heh, heh, heh."

Amazing what you can think is funny all by yourself after fighting cobwebs and musty books for that long.

I set that book into the usable section.

"What's this one? Oh. *Romeo and Juliet."* I flipped through the dusty pages. "Romeo, Romeo, wherefore art thou?" I began in a high voice. I switched to a deeper tone, "Down here in the bushes, stupid—"

I jumped as something brushed my neck. "Aaack! Killer spider!"

Then I gritted my teeth as I settled on solid ground and caught my balance. "Jooooeel," I said in my deepest, most threatening voice.

"I sent him down," called Mrs. Reynolds before I could get my fingers around his throat. "Thought you might need a break."

Joel smiled.

"No ma'am. I don't need a break. It's only been a couple days in this hole. I'm sure I can go another week."

She laughed as she descended the stairs, ducking beneath two large webs. "It's not that bad. You must nearly be done."

My face grew hot with redness. "Well, actually . . . "

She reached me and clucked disapproval at what she saw. "Only five boxes?"

I winced. "I, um, keep getting distracted. Looking through old books and checking the names of people who took them out years ago. You wouldn't believe some of the things I learned."

"But only five boxes? There are at least another twenty."

"Is your husband's name Tom?"

The change of subject slowed her briefly. "Yes, it is. Why?"

"Thought so. I'll work faster, I promise."

I went back to the boxes and hummed tunelessly.

"Ricky Kidd!" Mrs. Reynolds demanded. "Why did you want to know?"

"No reason." I paused. "Lots to do here. I guess I shouldn't waste time just talking."

I dropped a book near Joel's toe. Accident, of course. The spine of the book made a satisfying *thunk* that sent Joel a yard sideways. He dusted off his tiny knees in disgust, picked the book up, and glared at me.

How could I know he was there, I rehearsed smugly in my mind, *the little guy is always sneaking up on me*. I looked around for a book big enough to send him running.

"Ricky Kidd," Mrs. Reynolds' voice grew insistent. "There *must* be a reason for that question."

"Question?" I huffed with the exertion of moving boxes.

"Turn around, you rascal," she said to me.

I did. Joel was already gone. With the book. Which now meant I could only take four others home as a reward for this work.

"Now look me straight in the eye. Why did you want to know if my husband's name was Tom?"

"Oh. That. Well, I found a book he renewed every two weeks for ten times in a row."

"And?"

"It was in good condition. He must have treated it real nice the entire five months he had it."

"Not was it in good shape." She almost stamped one of her high heeled shoes. "What was the book called?"

I shuffled my feet. "It was a long time ago, I'm sure, not that important . . ."

"Spit it out."

I coughed delicately. *"The Teenaged Boy's Guidebook on How to Talk to Girls.* Or something like that. It was pretty old-fashioned."

Her mouth dropped.

"Did girls really wear dumb dresses like the pictures in the book showed?"

Her mouth snapped shut. Then she began to giggle.

"Tommy, Tommy, Tommy. That crazy little twerp," she said with affection as she smiled at the far wall. I had a hard time picturing her husband as a little twerp. He was huge, had no hair, and wore thick-rimmed glasses that made him look like a hoot owl.

Her smile grew as she continued. "That explains why he spent our first five dates talking about the opera, and another five on the advance of science. It drove me nuts. Especially because he knew nothing about either subject and *I* knew he couldn't say enough about cars and football to anyone else."

Her smile became a giggle, and then a full laugh until she stopped abruptly. "Where is that book? This has *got* to be our secret."

I cleared my throat again. *Here comes the tricky part.* "Actually, I've already put it in my pile to take home."

It took her a moment to catch on. "You've, you've . . ."

I nodded. "You did promise me five books of my choice."

I quickly moved to another box and grunted with the effort of moving it. I began my tuneless hum. And waited.

"Ricky Kidd, you shameless scamp!" She didn't know whether to get mad or to laugh. "Trying to blackmail me!"

"Blackmail!" I hoped my voice sounded hurt. I tried the line that I had been rehearsing for an hour. "That never crossed my mind. I just thought if that book helped him meet someone nice like you, I sure could use it when I get older too."

Then I faced her, and tried one of the honey grins that Mike always uses.

She shook her head in mock disgust. "All right," she sighed. "How much do you want for the book?"

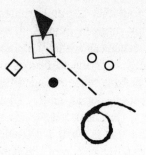

"Twelve cans of soda," Mike said with admiration as he joined me outside the city hall. "I thought you told me you were broke."

"I was," I said. "Would you believe Mrs. Reynolds liked my work so much, she gave me some money and sent me home early?" *Besides, telling Mike you're broke is the only safe statement to make whenever he inquires about money.*

"Yes," I continued. "All that's left is next Saturday morning. They'll be selling those books in the afternoon after I finish."

Mike continued to eye the cans of soda dangling from a plastic strap from my hand. I also carried two bags of red licorice.

"That's a lot of soda," he said. "I've got a great idea."

I shook my head. "Your last idea got us into this mess. It's three o'clock. Enough time to help Ralphy with the fence, and let him share this soda."

Mike shrugged.

We cut across the park between the city hall and the library. It was only two blocks more to the three-story house where Old Lady Bugsby lived. As we walked, Mike described in great detail the agony of scrubbing floors, then speculated on the horrors of the waxing which he had to do the next Saturday.

I told him about the mountains of boxes, but not about a book on how to talk to girls. After all, a promise is a promise.

It took great will power for each of us not to crack open a soda as we walked, but it wasn't far to join Ralphy, and when you share with friends, you should do it right. Like waiting until you can celebrate the loot together.

"Hey, Ralphy," Mike shouted as soon as we were remotely within hearing range. "Knock off the painting. We've got a surprise for you!"

Naturally, Mike made it sound like he'd helped me get the soda.

It didn't surprise me to see as much white paint on Ralphy as on the tall fence which surrounded Old Lady Bugsby's house.

His cheeks grinned white splotches at us as he noticed the soda.

"All right, Ricky! How'd you guess I was thirsty."

Mike put up a silencing arm. "Exactly how thirsty?"

I should have heard warning bells at the casual tone of his question.

"Real thirsty. This fence is a killer."

"Thirsty enough for a chugalug drinking contest?"

I interrupted. "No way, Mike. I can see right through that one. You're going to use the contest as a way to drink as much of this soda as possible."

"Chicken?" He smirked. "We'll have a race. First one to drink two cans gets his work done next week by the other two."

"I'm real, real thirsty," Ralphy told me with approval. "And it'll still leave you with six cans to take home."

I groaned. Why was it that Saturdays brought out the worst of Mike's restlessness?

Before they could move, I set the soda down, grabbed one, and in a quick motion popped the tab and started drinking.

"Cheater!" Mike shouted with glee. He swooped down, barely beating Ralphy to the cans.

"Aaack!" Ralphy howled with equal glee as he dove for a cola.

I ignored them. The bubbles burned my throat so badly that my eyes were already watering.

I stopped to gulp for breath. "Id's in my nose!"

That didn't distract them. Their eyes bulged like frogs with the effort of their swallowing.

"Hah!" Mike shouted. "One down."

Ralphy paused and hiccupped. "N-n-no fair. You sp-spilled h-hic-alf."

I grabbed the second can and nearly broke my thumbnail trying to crack it open. Already my stomach was ready to explode. *Why do we do these things?*

Mike gurgled a grin through a mouthful of cola.

I gasped. My throat and eyes and nose and mouth felt like they were all trying to escape out the back of my head. But I was not going to lose.

"Done!"

"Done!"

"D-d-hic-done!"

Mike began to roll with laughter. "A dead tie. You should have seen you guys!"

"You lo-hic-ooked worse," Ralphy accused.

I tried to remain dignified. But it was impossible. Not with cola all over my shirt and two friends busting themselves on the ground with the sheer glee of doing something crazy and unexpected.

My laughter made my stomach so weak, I couldn't stand either. But when I stopped to clear the tears from my eyes, I noticed something that sobered me in a big hurry.

Old Lady Bugsby. Head to toe in a black dress. Narrow nose and lips pursed in disapproval.

"Hmmph," she said with the piercing coldness of a north wind. Her dark clothing emphasized the gauntness of the dried-out wrinkles etched into the skin of her face. Brown age spots covered the backs of her hands. But despite her mean oldness, she stood strong and steady.

We stood quickly and tried brushing the grass off our clothes.

"Hmmph," she repeated. "So this is how you show you're sorry. I'm only glad my dear father isn't here today to see how little respect you have for him. First the statue. Now this. I should have known you'd treat your punishment in this way."

Ralphy opened his mouth to apologize. *"Hic!"* he said.

Old Lady Bugsby spun on her heels and marched away.

"Good going," Mike whispered to Ralphy.

"I di-hic-dn't mean it!"

Then Ralphy began hiccuping in a quick ticktock beat that reminded me of a grandfather clock.

His eyes grew wide. "I-hic-can't-hic-st-hic-st-hic-op!"

We watched him for five minutes and waited for the hiccupping to end. It didn't.

"We should call a doctor," Mike finally said.

Ralphy shook his head wildly.

"We don't need to," I said. "I know a remedy that works for sure."

"Wha-hic-at's that, Ri-hic-ky?"

"Hang upside down and drink some more."

"I think I heard that too," Mike said.

"No hic-way. I'm not th-hic-at stup-hic-id."

I'd already been stupid enough to get in a pop drinking contest. There seemed to be no reason to stop now. I demonstrated.

"Look," I said. I stood on my hands alongside the fence and carefully fit my feet into the spaces between the planks. Then I lifted my hands from the ground so that I hung by my feet from the top of the fence.

"A couple of chugalugs in this position, and you'll be like new." I gave him a doctorly, upside-down smile. My face was barely inches off the ground as I twisted to look upward.

"I-hic don't kn-hic-ow," he said.

We didn't have a chance to find out if my method would work. Lisa Higgins walked around the corner.

It seems she always catches me doing something stupid, and I couldn't think of anything stupider than hanging by my feet.

I tried to kick loose and only wedged my shoes farther into the gap between the planks.

"Hi guys," she said as she came closer.

Mike and Ralphy—the rat finks—stepped aside to give her a better view. Ralphy's hiccup pace doubled at her smile.

I wriggled again. Something felt like it was loosening.

"Whatever you're doing," Lisa said to me, "I'm not surprised."

I grunted and kicked harder.

That's when Joel darted out from behind a nearby tree and squeezed between Mike and Lisa as they admired me in my stuck position.

"Have your book back," Joel announced. "It's broken."

The fence creaked.

Joel placed the book into my hands before I could react.

It was broken. The cover was split and torn in both directions from where the spine had earlier thunked the floor beside his feet.

Before I could drop the book to free my hands, two things happened. With the book upside down, a piece of paper fell from a gap between the cover and the book itself.

It fluttered to the ground inches from my eyes.

A piece of parchment with bold letters.

GOLD SHALL BE THE REWARD
TO THE ONE WHO SEARCHES HARD

I barely had time to realize that it was a map before the second thing happened.

The planks of the old fence crashed down on top of me.

"That was Ethel Bugsby on the telephone," Mom said as she returned to the dining room table.

Outside, it was already dark, the way evening comes early in the fall.

I gulped as Mom sat. Not because of the mouthful of turkey sandwich. Because of fear.

"Does she want to put us in jail again?" I said after nearly choking.

"No, dear. She didn't even comment about the boards falling from her fence. Though why she couldn't figure it out by the rip in your pants and that bruise on your head is beyond me."

Joel clucked sympathy with a mouthful of bread.

He returned his eyes to the table when I glared at him. It's pretty bad when your six-year-old brother thinks he needs to feel sorry for you. Now, Lisa Higgins with a cold, damp cloth to wipe away the blood, that's another story, one that had gone an extra ten minutes because of my expert groaning after they pulled me out from under the fence boards.

I coughed. "Well, I did say that Ralphy and Mike did a good job putting it together before she came back to check the painting."

"Yes, dear," Mom said with mild irony. "You *are* such a saint to confess to us."

"Notice Ricky didn't confess to *her*," Dad said. "Of course, I remember her when I was growing up, and she was quite the old grouch then too."

"*Samuel.*" Mom tried to put shocked anger into her voice.

Dad shrugged and grinned.

"So why did Old Lady—I mean Miss Bugsby—just call?" I asked.

Mom sighed. "She says the old paint still shows through."

"We gave it two coats," I protested.

Dad resurfaced from his double-decker sandwich and snorted. "She probably used the cheapest paint possible."

He caught Mom's glare and remembered he wasn't supposed to think the slingshot had been funny. "But, of course, Ricky, if you guys hadn't fired that watermelon in the first place . . ."

I decided a quick subject change would be a good idea.

"Isn't she rich?" I asked.

"Extremely," Dad said.

"Then why is she so cheap?"

Dad set his knife down on the tablecloth, careful under Mom's watchful eyes to wipe the mayonnaise off it first.

"It's funny you should ask," he said in his thoughtful tone, the one I enjoy because he uses it to talk to me like I should be old enough to think things through. "Money does strange things to people."

"It's the root of all evil," I said, matching his thoughtful tone.

He shook his head. "The *love* of money is the root of all evil. That's an important distinction. Money itself is fine. It bought this food we're eating. It bought this house we use for shelter. Our clothes. It supports the church."

Mom knew that Dad was just warming up. She smiled.

"In our society money is a method for us to have and enjoy

the good things that God provides. But money, like many of the blessings available to us, can also be misused."

"Like Miss Bugsby does."

"Yes. When you have a lot, it should be shared freely."

Mom interrupted. "Don't judge Ethel too harshly, Samuel. One, that's between her, her conscience, and God. Two, she had a difficult life. She was an only child and her father ignored her for money. Everybody knows she's a little funny in that area, the way she sometimes thinks she's talking to him and stuff like that. All she wanted from him was love and he was a cr—".

She stopped herself and chose her words more carefully. ". . . her father was twisted when it came to money. All he wanted was more and more. I'm sad to say that he truly loved money. And it showed in the way he treated his family."

"Um, are those stories about him burying the gold true?"

Dad kept a straight face. "Sure, Ricky. I think he left most of it in our garden. Why don't you dig it up and check?"

I shook my head. "Yesterday you said it needed hoeing before winter set in. You're just trying to fool me into doing it for you."

"That's my son—smart as a whip," he told Mom.

"What about a map?" I persisted. "Maybe if someone found a map that he left behind in an old book."

Mom giggled at Dad. "He's your son, all right. The same one who wants to be a writer. . . . " She turned her smile on me. "Where do you come up with these ideas?"

"He was at the library, Stephanie. Stacking old books."

"It's true!" I said. "I found a map."

Dad pushed some lettuce onto his sandwich. "Sure, son. How many of those books are you trying to get me to buy?"

"Pardon me?"

"You dig up my garden looking for his gold. I'll buy those old books looking for more treasure maps." He shook his head. "I was born yesterday, but not last night."

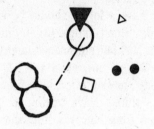

"Your parents didn't believe you either, Ralphy?"

He shook his head no and hiccuped.

"Mine neither," Lisa said. She shook her head in sympathy at Ralphy. "Is it true every teacher in every one of your classes sent you to see the school nurse today?"

He nodded his head yes and hiccuped again.

It was Monday afternoon after school. We were crunching our way through the leaves of the park near the library, about to meet with Mike to discuss the treasure map.

Trees threw long spiked shadows across our paths. Beside us, a tall, thick hedge quivered with the faint whistle of wind.

"I could barely sleep this weekend just thinking about the map and a treasure," I said. "To think that somewhere nearby is—"

Lisa clutched my arm as the hedge beside us parted.

"Aaaaagggghhhh!" I heard a voice screaming wildly. I then realized it was mine but that didn't stop it from happening again. "Aaaaggghh!"

The hedge burst open completely. The monster in front of us was huge, at least twice my height, and looked like a mixture between a gorilla and a bear and a werewolf, and it continued to stagger right toward us!

With my usual brilliance and quick action, I shoved Lisa behind me and gave my best defense. I screamed again.

I grabbed Ralphy as he stepped forward beside me. I couldn't believe his braveness.

The monster lurched a step closer and roared anger!

"Hic—hi, Mike," Ralphy said without enthusiasm. "Nice tr-hic-try."

"Nuts," a familiar voice said from the horrible face.

Mike!

He staggered closer and leaned a paw downward on Ralphy's shoulder. "Give me support, pal, while I get off these stilts."

Mike Andrews?

"Nice try!?! Stilts!?!" I shouted. My legs still shook and my head pounded from the way my heart had rocketed into sonic gear.

"Sorry," Mike said as he stumbled down and removed his mask. He concentrated on unzipping his suit and pulling out the stilts. "I was just trying to scare away Ralphy's hiccups."

In reply, Ralphy hiccupped.

All of my skin still tingled from the adrenaline that had gushed in a single burst. "Brilliant idea, Mr. Psychiatrist," I accused. "You could have given someone a heart attack."

"I said 'sorry.' I didn't mean to scare *you* half to death."

"Me? Hah. I was thinking about Lisa."

Lisa giggled.

Mike kept stripping away the fake fur. "Neat costume, huh. I got it at half price. Maybe next time, Ralphy."

"That's OK," he managed to say without hiccuping. "It's the thought that counts." *Then* he hiccupped.

* * * * * * * *

After we promised to whisper, Mrs. Reynolds directed us to a table in the far corner of the library.

Little did she know how quiet we wanted to be. After all, we had a precious secret. There was no way we would talk loudly enough for someone to hear us ten feet away, let alone over by the newspaper section where two old men were reading the dailies. I recognized them both from all the time they spend hanging around Mr. Breeton's barber shop. One has squinty eyes buried in a lot of wrinkles, and the other I always remember for the way his thumbs and fingers are yellow from all the cigarettes he smokes.

"Let's plan our course of action," I said softly.

The day before, Sunday, had been, of course, a church day. We had not been able to get together to discuss the map until now.

"You've got the map?" Mike asked just as softly. "I dreamed about it all weekend."

I nodded, then reached into my school knapsack and pulled out the old book with the torn cover. I took the carefully folded map out from the middle of the pages.

Dark lines showed clearly on the yellow paper. It was torn down one side, as if someone had ripped it in half.

"We should make some photocopies," I whispered as I smoothed the map on the table.

Lisa dug into her purse and handed Mike some quarters. He nodded, took the map, and left the table.

HIC!

It almost echoed through the hush around us.

"Hold your breath for ten minutes," Mrs. Reynolds called from the checkout desk.

Ralphy took a deep breath and obediently plugged his nose.

I sighed. For a computer genius, sometimes he doesn't think.

"After ten minutes," I pointed out, "your hiccups will be gone but so will you."

"Oh."

He kept his hand over his mouth to muffle more hiccups.

Mike returned and passed a copy around for each of us. "Let no one else see these," he warned gravely. "Our parents might not believe us, but others will. The last thing we want is everyone in town trying to beat us to the treasure."

We all nodded yes — Ralphy hicked once — and looked closely at our maps.

In bold lettering at the top were the words that had mesmerized me shortly before my upside-down fall from the fence.

GOLD SHALL BE THE REWARD
TO THE ONE WHO SEARCHES DEEP AND HARD
YET START THROUGH THE SOOT
FOR THE DISCOVERY OF THE LOOT

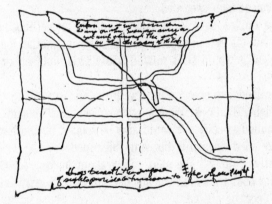

(THINGS BENEATH THE SURFACE OF SIGHT
PROVIDE A TREASURE TO THE ONE WHO SEES IT RIGHT)

We all stared hard at the map.

"Soot, soot," Lisa said. "Buried in a fireplace? Think, guys."

Nothing resulted except Ralphy's muffled hics.

"I was afraid of this," I said. "All weekend I tried to make sense of it, but couldn't. If you guys can't ... "

"Even without the rip down one edge, I would guess that part of the map is missing," Lisa said. "I can recognize some of the landmarks, but they don't make sense."

"May-hic-be the other piece of the map is hidden in an-hic-other book," Ralphy suggested.

"I was afraid you'd guess that too. This isn't going to be an easy search, is it?"

I picked up the heavy book with its faded pages and read aloud its title. "Where do we look next. This one is called *The Pioneers of Jamesville.*"

There was a moment of silence. Lisa took the book from me and flipped the cover open.

"Maybe in its sequel," Mike suggested.

Lisa raised one eyebrow.

"Hang on," I said. "He may be on to something. If Fred Bugsby left the missing piece of the map in another book, it's only logical it would be a related book. Title, subject, or maybe author."

Lisa raised her eyebrow in my direction.

"All right, Sherlock. What's your suggestion?" I said.

She smiled sweetly. "It could also be related in another way."

Ralphy tried speaking, but only hiccuped.

"Exactly, Ralphy," she said. "How about looking for the map in another book that Fred Bugsby used to own? Regardless of the title, subject, or author."

She handed me the book, open to the inside cover. In large letters, a stamp said, "This belongs to the library of Fred Bugsby."

I didn't say a word. Instead, I stood quietly and walked a straight line to the checkout counter.

"Mrs. Reynolds?"

"Glad to see Ralphy's hiccups have stopped rattling my dentures," she replied. Then giggled.

"Good one, ma'am. I've got a question about those old books."

"This should be interesting," she said. "Did you have another one on dating to sell me for ten dollars?"

I coughed. "Actually, I'm wondering where they came from. I think one on Jamesville's pioneering days had a stamp from Fred Bugsby's private library."

"Yes," she said. "Old Lady—I mean Miss Bugsby tried selling us a few boxes of them a couple years back, and was not pleased when I said we would be happy to accept them as a donation. Of course, she insisted we go to her place to pick them up."

"Thank you," I said over my shoulder as I scooted back.

"Bingo!" I told Lisa. "There's a few more boxes of books in the basement from Fred's library."

"We can buy them," Mike said. "As you finish sorting the boxes this Saturday, set aside all of Fred Bugsby's books. They're real cheap, right, Ricky? We'll buy all of them, and take the covers apart later!"

"For once," I said with satisfaction, "I can't see any trouble coming out of one of your ideas. Lisa? Ralphy?"

They agreed with me.

"Except," I said. "I don't want to wait until Saturday to sort. Maybe all of you can help me tomorrow after school."

They groaned.

"Hey," I protested. "You guys don't think I'm trying to get out of work? This is a treasure hunt."

It took a little longer for them to agree, but they did.

I rubbed my hands with satisfaction. "Terrific. Remember, if we keep this our secret, absolutely nothing can stop—"

"Gold! Gold! This has got to be Bugsby's missing gold!" It was the old man with squinty eyes who had been reading a newspaper.

"Gold shall be the reward for the one who searches hard!" He shouted as he held a piece of paper high in the air. *"It's a treasure map."*

Lisa sighed.

Ralphy's hiccuping tripled.

Mike looked at me in horror.

"He wouldn't happen to be standing beside the photocopier?" I asked Mike.

Mike winced.

"The same photocopier," I continued, "with the original treasure map left on top?"

Mike winced again.

"Maybe," I said slowly. "With the wind behind you and no flat tires, you could be 50, maybe 60, miles from here by dark."

I reached for his throat, but Lisa beat me to it.

It was exactly two weeks and three and three-quarter hours after the slingshot accident that we headed toward the exact spot where that watermelon had smashed a statue in front of the library. Only *this* Saturday, as Mike and Ralphy and I approached the street corner that turned to the library, my heart wasn't doing flip-flops of terror at what damage we might find.

"You've got the list of books we need to buy, right, Ricky?" Mike asked.

"Have I said 'yes' to that question five times already today?" He nodded.

"Then it's a safe bet I'll say 'yes' again, isn't it."

"You don't have to be grouchy. After all, the rest of us saved you hours of work going through those books to get them ready for this afternoon's sale."

"Grouchy? Me?" I snorted. "You're the one who gave away a treasure map by leaving it on the photocopier."

"That again," Mike groaned. "If you bring it up one more time—"

Ralphy, walking behind us as usual, suddenly placed a hand on each of our shoulders and spun us around to face him. Something unusual burned on his face. Anger.

"You guys listen to me," he said in a tight, quiet voice. "I've spent this entire week listening to the both of you argue. It's getting so bad that it doesn't even sound like you're friends."

"But Ralphy, this gold could be worth a fortune and because of Mike everybody in town now knows—"

"Don't interrupt me again," he said with the same quiet anger as he grabbed my shirt and pulled me closer.

I snapped my mouth shut. I had never seen Ralphy like this. He seemed to be two inches taller and fifty pounds stronger. His grip on my shirt did not relax.

"I don't particularly care if we find that gold," he said as he stared into my eyes. "Not if it busts up friends that mean more to me than any fortune. If it's going to be like this as we go looking, you can count me out."

He dropped his hand from my shirt and stared at the back of his knuckles.

When he spoke again, the anger had been replaced with a deep sadness. "In fact, you can count me out right now. Anything that makes me mad enough to physically threaten my best friend is something I don't need."

He began to walk away. "Sorry, guys," he said. "Call me when we can all remember there's more important things than money."

That's how he left us. Walking away. Shirt hanging out of the back of his pants. Hair sticking straight up. And a resigned slouch to his shoulders.

I looked at Mike.

Mike looked at me.

"Actually," I said to Mike, "leaving the map on the photocopier was a great idea. It'll just make the treasure hunt more of a challenge."

"Don't sweet-talk me," he replied. "I still think you're a grouchy dough head." Then he dazzled me with a hundred watt grin that erased a week's worth of fighting.

"Dough head? Dough head?" I asked. "You're too dumb to think of a better insult than that?"

He shrugged. "Not on short notice."

We both yelled at the same time. "Hey Ralphy! Dough head! Get back here!"

He turned quickly and grinned, as if he had been waiting for something like that from us. When he reached us, I suddenly realized something about the lecture he had just delivered.

"Ralphy! You got so mad that your hiccups stopped!"

He smiled shyly and seemed his normal size again. "Only *HIC* my body remembered them again."

Ten seconds later, regular as a drip from a tap, another hiccup hit him. It was lost, however, in Mike's yelp of surprise as we rounded the corner to the library.

* * * * * * * *

"Half of the town is here," Lisa informed us, raising her voice above the noise of the crowd surrounding us. "It's obvious not much is secret about the map or how we found it."

She was right.

We had difficulty forcing our way through the lines of people to find the tables of books in front of the library. It was so busy that the large cardboard signs with felt-penned prices that Mrs. Reynolds had perched among the stacks were now scattered on the ground.

Even Mr. McKinnley had ventured an appearance. "I don't see any Germans here," he was saying in a quavery voice to Mrs. McKinnley's broad back. "That phone call of mine must have stopped that bombing attack in a big hurry."

She ignored him and shoved past two other people to get at some of the old books.

The babbling around us grew louder. Ralphy and Lisa were separated from us by the people pushing and shoving.

"Mike!" I hollered into his ear. "Do you remember which pile we made for those books?"

"This way."

Three steps later, I tapped him on the shoulder.

He turned around.

I pointed behind me.

Squinty Eyes and Yellow Fingers, the two old men from the library, were following me so closely I could feel breath on the back of my neck.

They looked at both of us and shrugged. "Hey," Squinty Eyes said, "it's a free world, ain't it?"

Mike and I stared at them, unable to think of a reply.

"Here's the dollar I owe you," Mike finally said to me.

I was too surprised at the sudden change of subject to ask what he was doing. I reached for the bill he offered from his fingertips.

"Nuts," Mike said as the dollar fell and floated to the ground. Then I understood as he backed away.

Squinty Eyes and Yellow Fingers both fought to reach it first.

Mike melted into the crowd in front of me. I took a different direction. Three minutes later, we met in front of a table near the library steps.

Mrs. Reynolds waved at me from behind a small cash register. She was too busy making change to do much else. I waved in return, but kept my eyes moving to search for the books that had belonged to Fred Bugsby.

"They should be right here," I said. "All twelve of them."

Then I noticed Old Lady Bugsby watching us from the side of the crowd with the cool smile of a cat in front of a mouse hole.

"Mike," I said from the corner of my mouth. "This doesn't look good."

"Huh?"

"Trouble in front and to our left."

"Joel?" he asked without looking.

"Worse."

He noticed immediately. "She's headed this way," he said tersely. "If it's about the fence, I'll be happy to tell her it was your fault."

"Thanks, pal."

She stopped on the other side of the table and crooked a long finger at us. "Over here," she said.

"Us?"

"Of course, you silly gooses." She showed us her teeth in what she probably thought was a smile.

As we edged our way around the table to meet her, Mike whispered, " 'Silly gooses'? And you thought 'dough head' was a dumb name."

I didn't have a chance to reply.

Old Lady Bugsby dropped her fake smile and got to business. "How much for the book?"

As she spoke, she moved away from the tables so that it was easier to hear her. Each movement she made was with a rigid straightness.

"Book?" I asked.

Her gray eyes were almost hypnotic and we found ourselves moving with her.

"Don't be ridiculous," she snapped. "Everybody in town knows about it by now. The book that had half a map to the gold."

"We'd rather not sell it, ma'am," Mike said quietly.

She turned on Mike with an abrupt fierceness. "Nobody denies me anything. What's your price." It did not come out like a question.

Mike and I both squirmed. We were not used to saying no to grown-ups.

"Fine," she said after some silence. "Keep your book. I've

already got a copy of what you found in it. Rest assured I'll find the missing half on my own."

We still said nothing.

The wrinkles around her high cheekbones tightened as she glared at us. "As you can see by this crowd, you two weren't the only ones who guessed the secret would be in another book."

She dropped her voice to a hiss. "Like idiots, you both thought there would be no competition at the book sale. Quite wrong, weren't you."

I flinched under her gaze.

She paused and put the tip of one bony finger under my chin.

"You see, Sherlock Junior, nobody else here—not even you— was smart enough to show up two days early and buy books ahead of time. Except for me."

"But—" Mike began from beside me.

"In other words, I want to thank you both." She ignored Mike and lifted her finger slightly, enough pressure to tilt my face so that her eyes could bore into mine. "If you hadn't sorted my father's books so neatly, I would have had to buy every book in that dreary library basement just to be sure."

The slate gray of her eyes narrowed as her voice rose with cold triumph. "As it is, boys, I only had to pay for twelve."

Standing in your kitchen with a friend's ear pinched between the thumb and forefinger of your left hand and with a spoonful of peanut butter in your right hand is not the way to be found when someone like Lisa Higgins walks in through the back porch.

"Hi guys," she said without surprise. "Still no cure?"

"You *could* knock," Mike said. He was grumpy because his hair and his new shirt were still plastered wet.

"I heard yelling."

"Joel was hiding under the sink to listen to us," I explained. "He decided to come out while Mike was filling a jug of water. The cupboard door banged Mike's knee and he jumped a mile."

Ralphy hiccupped and giggled.

"Some gratitude, Ralphy. I *was* getting the water for you."

"Well, this remedy ought to be a good one," Lisa said. "Especially from a crew of rocket scientists like you guys. A watermelon slingshot one week, medical history the next."

"Hah, hah," Mike said. "I'll have you know this works on the scientific theory of acupressure."

I was studying the second hand on my watch. *Three, two, one . . . HIC!* Ralphy didn't miss a beat as Mike kept explaining.

"We pinch a pressure point on his ear which hits the right

nerve just as he tries swallowing a mouthful of peanut butter and water. My mother said her aunt's grandmother said it was foolproof."

"Meaning even fools can't miss?"

Mike tried a glare which didn't dim Lisa's smile for a second. So he turned to me. "Ready?"

I nodded and pinched the bottom of Ralphy's earlobe and when he yelped I popped the peanut butter in his mouth. As I pulled the empty spoon free, Mike poured the water and just to be safe, pinched Ralphy's other ear.

Ralphy winced and swallowed hard.

I resumed studying my watch. *Three, two, one . . . HIC!*

"Nuts," Mike said. "We'll give it one more try."

"I liked the chocolate cure better," Ralphy said as he rubbed his ears. "Sure, it was expensive but—eep!"

There was Joel, suddenly among us with a mirror and comb. He offered them upward to Mike.

"Joel's trying to tell you that your hair's messy," I said. Years of aggravation had made me an expert on Joel. "It means he's sorry for scaring you into spilling the water on yourself."

"Fine." Mike set the mirror on the table. "First Ralphy's miracle cure."

Lisa coughed to get attention. Joel took advantage of the distraction to snatch back the mirror and comb before disappearing.

"Wouldn't you guys rather find a buried treasure?" she asked.

"Sh-hic-ure. But everybody in town is looking."

"Besides," I added, "with all of the other books, Old Lady Bugsby's got the best chance now."

Lisa gave us the look she reserves for particularly dumb dummies. "Less than two hours after the book sale, and you've already given up."

"Not exactly," I protested. "Look at the kitchen table."

She turned her head to see. "A jar of peanut butter, seven chocolate bar wrappings . . . "

" . . . three copies of the map," I finished. "And the pioneer book opened for possible clues. We were thinking hard, only Mike remembered another cure so we thought we'd take a break."

"Did you think about Old Lady Bugsby and the other books?" Lisa asked.

Her tone of voice suggested she knew something.

"Of course." I could still feel the sharp edge of that fingernail under my chin.

"When did she say she bought them?"

"Ricky told you at the sale," Mike interrupted. "Two days ago. Right after we did all that work to sort the rest of the books."

"Exactly. Two days ago. Do you think she's waiting until tonight to slice open all the covers and look for the other map?"

"No way," Mike said. "She's so hungry for money that—"

I waved him quiet as it hit me. "Mike. Why would she be so anxious to buy our pioneer book if—like everybody else in town —she's already got a copy of our map, and—unlike anybody in town—has already searched all the other twelve old books for more clues?"

Silence as it dawned on Mike.

More silence as he grinned at Ralphy and as Ralphy grinned back at him. The silence was broken only by the ticking of the kitchen clock and two of Ralphy's hiccups.

"Old Lady Bugsby wants our pioneer book," Mike said slowly, "because she still thinks she needs something from it."

I nodded. "In other words, she thinks the secret can be figured out from what we have. Something that none of the treasure seekers have but us."

Mike rubbed his hands. "What an awesome conclusion. Just call us geniuses, pal!"

Lisa sighed.

It took until Monday after school to begin our next step because it took until Monday after school before we could all meet at the town library.

"Hi, gang. Hi, Hic Ralphy," Mrs. Reynolds called from a stack of books as we all walked in.

Ralphy hiccuped and turned red.

Mrs. Reynolds chuckled and pointed to an open table in the corner of the library.

As soon as Mike, Ralphy, Lisa, and I sat down, the men that I thought of as Squinty Eyes and Yellow Fingers moved from their usual position by the newspaper racks, left their shabby coats behind, and sat at the table behind us.

So much for a treasure hunting discussion. How do you tell grown-ups to leave?

"Here's a list of books that might have clues," Lisa whispered loudly.

I noticed that each man reached for a pen. I tried to wave Lisa silent.

She ignored me. "Notice all of them were around while Fred Bugsby was still alive."

Click. Click. Their pens were ready.

I shook my head wildly. Then placed a finger in front of my mouth. It didn't work.

"Gone with the Wind. Tom Sawyer. Pride and Prejudice."

I groaned. "Not so loud, Lisa!" This time, however, I made sure my voice carried clearly.

"And all of the books by that philosopher Plato," she finished.

With a double scrape, each of the two men pushed their chairs back.

"Hey, that's not fair," I protested. "You were listening."

"Cry to your momma, kid," Squinty Eyes crowed as they stood. "All's fair in love and war and treasure hunts."

"Yeah," Yellow Fingers chimed. "And don't think we'll be returning those books for a while neither."

They smiled smugly and headed toward the card catalog files. "Told you those kids were our best bet," Yellow Fingers said just before they were out of hearing range. "We'll get a good jump on everyone now."

We all looked at each other.

"Did I do OK, Ricky?" Lisa asked. "Those were the only old books I could think of. Mostly from my dad's bookshelf at home."

I grinned. "More than OK. For a minute I thought you wanted to read off the real list."

"I notice you didn't lie," Mike said. "All you said was that the books *might* have clues."

"Chances are *HIC* they might *not*," from, of course, Ralphy's corner.

With Squinty Eyes and Yellow Fingers gone, I could unfold the real list.

"Two things," I said. "One, if the missing part of the map was not in any of the covers of the books Old Lady Bugsby took home, there might be clues within the written parts. We can look for those clues in copies of the books."

"We'll have to read?" Mike asked with a pained expression.

"Yes, Mike. Your lips might get tired because you still read out loud, but everyone has to do their part."

"Hah. Hah."

"The second thing, Ricky?" Lisa asked.

"The titles themselves might give us clues. It's all I can think of at this point."

"You are reading the pioneer book cover to *HIC* cover, right?"

"You bet, Ralphy. When I finish, I'm giving it to Lisa. If she can't find anything significant, she's giving it to you. Last, Mike will go through it."

"And we'll keep staring at the map for hours in case it finally makes sense," Mike added. "Not a bad plan."

I nodded. "Each of us takes three books from this list. Scan them first for anything obvious. Then read through. We'll compare notes in a few days."

I read the list of the twelve other books that had come from Moth-Wallet Bugsby's library.

"*The Power of Positive Thinking* by Norman Vincent Peale. *Double Your Money in Six Months* by Wallace Jedson. *A Thesis on Laboratory Techniques* by James Kendall. *Modern Science in the Western World* by William Coosey . . . "

I finished the list, then thought out loud. "Six books on money, and six on science. I wonder if that means anything?"

Lisa and Mike shrugged.

We copied down our three titles each, and sprang into action.

Too soon, all of us returned to the table.

"I couldn't *HIC* find mine," Ralphy said. "There were empty spots, but no *HIC* books."

Mike and Lisa reported the same.

"Me too." I doubt I managed to hide my glumness. "I hope Old Lady Bugsby didn't take them all out on Saturday."

"Ask Mrs. Reynolds," Mike whispered. "She's the one who gave you ten dollars."

If you only knew why, I thought, *you'd send Lisa.*

Ralphy hiccuped, a reminder of how much soda that money had bought.

I approached the checkout counter.

"I'm sure glad you have a good sense of humor, Mrs. Reynolds," I said. "Did your husband enjoy the book on dating?"

She shook her head with mock sadness. "So what do you want from me now, you rascal."

"Mrs. Reynolds," I said with as much grief as possible. "How could you think I want—"

She shushed me quiet and reached behind the counter. "Is this what you're looking for?"

The cover showed bold letters. *The Power of Positive Thinking.*

I gaped. "Yes! But how did—"

She brought some more books out. Eleven more. All the books we needed from the list.

"Ricky," she said in a more serious tone. "This treasure hunt thing is all over town. Frankly, I think it's a useless chase. Old Fred Bugsby would never let anyone have his money—even after being long dead. However—"

She paused and pushed a wisp of hair back.

". . . before the sale, Ethel Bugsby marched in here and demanded those old books back, waving a big check around. I couldn't think of a reason not to sell them to her, otherwise I would have kept them for you guys. I think it would be fun to be your age and search for clues to a lost treasure. So I wondered what I would do next if I were in your shoes if those old books had been snatched away from you and . . . "

She leaned forward and dropped her voice to a conspiracy level. " . . . and I'm glad to see I guessed right. I signed all of the same books out in your name. You've got them for the next two weeks."

I didn't know what to say except thanks. It makes you feel warm when grown-ups go to the effort of remembering what it was like when they were kids.

"Hang on," she said as I began to stumble backwards with the armful of books.

She walked around the counter and placed two more on top of the pile.

I staggered slightly.

"A medical book with folk cures for hiccups for poor Ralphy. And an up-to-date history book on Jamesville and area." She winked. "The only copy around. It's too bad for the other treasure hunters that you also signed it out for the next two weeks."

"Up-to-date history?"

"Of course. If you're looking for clues, you need to know more about Fred Bugsby, right? His biography is on pages 63 to 75. Look for people mentioned who are still alive today. They might have a thing or two to tell you."

Why hadn't I thought of that?

"A new car," I promised her. "When we find it, we're going to buy you a new car."

"Sure, Ricky," she said. "Make it a convertible."

She was still laughing to herself when I sat down at the table.

"Here they are, guys."

"Wow! She must *HIC* really like you, Ricky."

I shrugged. "Boyish charm, I guess."

Lisa snorted.

"No respect," I muttered, then proudly puffed out my chest as I held out the history book. "By the way, don't you agree that it'd be smart to research Fred Bugsby?"

Surprise crossed Lisa's face. "Good idea! Why hadn't I thought of that?"

"Never underrate guys," I told her gravely. "You never know what we'll come up with when you need it most."

"This is it, pal. Stonewall Sawyer's house. Twelve Park Street," Mike announced.

"I don't like it, Mike," I said. "It's something we have to do, but I wish we didn't. I mean, I can barely believe his family was once the richest in the entire county."

"It does seem creepy," Ralphy added.

Mike and I looked at him and waited.

"HIC!"

With that one finished—Ralphy still hiccuped with regularity, only farther apart and louder now—we began to study the yard and the small run-down house that was Number Twelve Park Street.

The fence in front of us was chest high, constructed of vertical slats of weathered and cracked wood. It sagged and dipped in various places along the entire length. Weeds reached through the slats for the sidewalk.

The yard itself seemed an obstacle course between the street and the house, which sat well back from view. A narrow unswept sidewalk wound among sprawling bushes and massive oak trees. The patchy grass that covered the ground between the trees and bushes was tall enough to show clumps of seed at the tips.

With a half hour already gone after the end of school, the late afternoon sun had begun to set directly behind the house. Long shadows cast the details of the front porch and shuttered windows into an ominous darkness.

Bang!

We jumped. Ralphy hiccupped.

"Just the screen door," I told them.

"We should just wait here on the sidewalk and watch," Mike suggested. "You know, preliminary research."

"Sure," I said. "Lisa's on her way. Maybe *she'll* go in later."

Mike straightened immediately. "Are you saying I'm scared?"

"Yup."

He didn't hesitate more than two seconds before pushing the gate open. "Come on, pal. We've got a treasure to find."

We took several slow steps. I was in the middle, bumping Mike and getting bumped from behind.

"Um, Ralphy? You can quit trying to hide inside my shirt."

"HIC."

A dozen more steps and we were more than halfway to the house. Even that close, it was impossible to decide if someone actually lived in it. Since it was an area of town we rarely visited, we knew little about the type of people who lived on the street.

"Um, Ricky?" Mike said as quietly as a person can speak. "I'm going to reach behind me to grab your arm. When I have it, back up very slowly and guide me in the direction of the nearest tree."

"Nice try," I said, chilled by the tone of his voice. "Anything to scare Ralphy from his hiccups."

Instead of replying, he moved his hand behind his back and felt gingerly for my arm.

It was enough movement for me to see over his shoulder.

Ralphy in turn saw over mine.

It's hard to say if the sneak-away method would have worked better than the sheer panic method. Either way, we didn't have a choice. A black dog the size of a lion was crouched behind a bush and staring midnight eyes in our direction. It rose and growled.

Ralphy screamed. Or Mike screamed. Or I screamed.

It was hard to tell who made the noise, and just as hard to tell who reached the oak tree first. It didn't matter. We flailed at each other and the rough bark as we scrambled and shouted and stepped on each other's hands in pursuit of as much space between us and the ground as possible.

When time snapped back to normal and we all noticed that our arms and legs were still attached to us instead of in the dog's mouth, Mike managed to stop heaving for breath long enough to say, "Don't even think that little puppy scared me. It's just that I believe in caution."

It waited directly below us. Most terrifying was its silence. It simply stared up at us with those glittering eyes. There appeared to be a leather harness system around its shoulders and enough room on its back for me to ride—had I been crazy enough to drop down and grab that harness.

"Sure, Mike," I panted in return. "Not scared at all. Then you'll unwrap your arms from my stomach?"

He let go of me and quickly reached for the trunk of the tree. The dog below us, massive head craned upward, growled at the sudden movement, then jumped high and snapped its teeth shut on about ten cubic feet of air.

"HIC!"

If this wasn't enough to cure Ralphy, I thought, *he's doomed to hiccups for the rest of his life.*

Before I could tell him that, Ralphy pointed down the street. I groaned.

* * * * * * * *

It's not often that I have a chance to watch Joel in action.

From our aerial position, however, I saw perfectly what I never manage to see when I'm on the ground being followed.

It seemed his feet never moved as he glided from one hiding spot to another. One second, kneeled beside a car. The next, straight up behind a tree trunk. Between, a cocking of the head as he tested the wind for sounds. And the entire time, his teddy bear secure in one hand.

Joel's infallible radar drew him closer and closer to Number Twelve Park Street—closer and closer to the front gate and the path of terror below us.

He scurried silently down the sidewalk. Each time he stopped, Joel somehow blended in with the fence slats.

Then, he peeked over the front of the gate.

He frowned, probably because we weren't visible as expected. I could almost hear him thinking, *I'm never wrong about these things. Where did they go?*

"Warn him, Ricky," Mike whispered hoarsely. "There's no way Joel can see this monster dog from where he's standing."

What a dilemma. *On one hand, if I kept my mouth shut, maybe Joel would learn a lesson and never follow us again. On the other hand, this dog was big enough to snap Joel in two. But on the first hand, Joel has a special charm with animals and would probably make friends with it. But on the second hand again, if Joel made friends with the same dog that treed the three of us, how stupid would we look?*

A single note of music—barely heard at first but rising in pureness—interrupted my complicated decision. It came from the darkness of the porch and the dog shifted to face the new sound.

Another long and haunting note followed softly.

The dog laid its huge body on the ground, and rested its chin between its paws.

Each new note seemed to arrive as a gift carried by the

autumn breeze. Those sounds drifted to us with a sweet clearness that sent shivers along the back of my neck. Then the single notes flowed to become a sad melody which filled me with the restless ache I'd feel when wild geese flew overhead late at night, honking their lonely cries of freedom to bring me out of sleep.

The music from the invisible player continued and grew, voicing wordless stories about loves and lives that any kid who has ever dreamed could understand without wondering how or why.

The dog below us settled and visibly sighed. I felt like doing the same under the spell of those long, sad notes.

Then the music trailed away so slowly it was hard to tell when it stopped and when the rustling of the wind in the leaves began.

"Wow," Mike whispered as if he had been afraid to break the new silence.

I was about to agree, then I looked down and nearly fell from the branch.

Joel!

He had his hand on the harness around the big dog's shoulder. Both of them were staring at the porch. I was reluctant to call and make any noise after the softness of that music.

"Blue," a voice called from the darkness. "Blue, you out there?"

The dog whined, then turned his head upward and licked Joel's hand.

"Come on in, boy." A chuckle. "What's the matter, Blue. Don't like my music after all these years?"

A muffled hic beside me, barely audible above the wind. I winced, but ignored Ralphy.

Joel absently scratched between the dog's ears as he too stared in the direction of the man's voice.

As the man appeared at the top of the steps, his voice grew concerned. "This isn't like you, boy. Tell me what's the matter."

Blue's whine grew deeper.

The man shuffled forward, wrapping an old jacket around his frail shoulders. It was our first look at Stonewall Sawyer. As he stepped into the last light of the afternoon, I could see he was compact and short, and definitely as old as Old Lady Bugsby. In sharp contrast to the round dark glasses perched on his nose, his hair was short and grizzled white. He leaned on a crooked cane and shuffled slowly down the steps.

His pants were shapeless black, and matched the vest that covered his trim upper body. He wore a white shirt with long sleeves that were carefully cufflinked into place.

"Blue!" His voice grew sharp with worry. "Answer me!"

Another whine, almost human.

The old man poked ahead of him with the cane as he turned to the sound of his dog. Then I realized what the harness meant. The old man was blind.

Now we were too embarrassed to say anything from the tree.

As Stonewall neared Blue, he tucked the cane under his left arm and reached ahead. "How come you don't move, Blue? You hurt?"

The love and sudden anguish in the old man's voice was almost enough to make me cry out.

Just as he reached his dog, Joel slipped sideways. Joel, of course, meant no harm to the old man. The dog sensed it and did nothing in reaction. Instead, Blue changed his pitch to a low grumbling in our direction.

"People," the old man said softly. "Where?"

He grabbed Blue's head with both hands. Blue pointed his jaw upward at us.

The old man dropped his hands. "In the tree!"

Stonewall peered upward, but instead of focusing his eyes on us, turned his face slightly to listen.

"You up there. Tell me your game."

Ralphy hiccupped obligingly.

Joel—standing within a foot of the old man—stared upward too, and his eyes widened in surprise to see all three of us crouched on the branch.

"Speak now," the old man commanded in a strong voice. "I know you're there."

Joel looked at the old man, looked at us, looked back at the old man, and frowned. I guessed that the frown meant Joel didn't realize Stonewall was blind and wondered why he didn't notice us, because he stood on his tiptoes to shout into the old man's ear.

"It's my brother!"

Joel's given me heart attacks the same way dozens of times before.

"YEEOOWWW!" Stonewall bellowed—much the same way I do.

The old man leapt straight up and managed to kick his legs wildly before landing on top of his dog. He shattered his cane against the sidewalk and finished with a sideways roll onto the unraked grass that left his jacket smeared with mud and his glasses pushed hard against his nose.

"Blue," Stonewall groaned directly into the sky. "You and me need to talk about security around here."

The knot in my stomach warned me that we had not made a good impression on our best lead to the buried treasure.

13

"What time is it?" Stonewall asked.

"Four-thirty," Lisa told him. "Is the tea everything I promised it would be?"

"Yes, ma'am. Not only do you sound like my late wife, you make tea exactly as good." He leaned forward, and sipped slowly. "See how I keep my hands around this cup? It's a habit I developed to keep my fingers warm during ... well ... sorry ... you didn't visit to hear an old man ramble on."

We were sitting in his front room. Except for Stonewall's chair, the furniture consisted of dull wooden coffee tables and mismatched straight-backed chairs. Stonewall's chair was faded red and so large it almost dwarfed him. Blue was asleep on the floor in front of him. He twitched, however, each time Ralphy hiccupped.

There were no pictures on the wall, no decorations or knick-knacks. I had nearly asked why until I remembered that Stonewall would never see them anyway. There was, of course, no television.

One thing did surprise me about the room. His music system. The speakers were nearly as tall as he was, and the components looked like the newest ones available. No wonder those notes had been so clear and beautiful. I told myself not to forget to ask him what compact disc he had been playing.

He sipped another mouthful of tea. "Oh, yes. Four-thirty. Kids like you must have suppers waiting. Therefore, I'm allowing this interview to last only until 5 P.M."

He paused and spoke in my direction. "On the condition you keep good hold of that brother of yours."

"Yes, sir," I said, tightening my grip on the teddy bear between my knees and on Joel's small fingers in my right hand.

I grinned at Mike. This was much better than we expected. If Lisa hadn't arrived just as the old man staggered to his feet, we'd probably still be in the tree, or worse, in jail. It took Lisa's sweetest convincing to get Stonewall to agree to a hot cup of tea and some apologetic company. Still, Mike, Ralphy, and I weren't completely happy. Lisa, after all, had caught us cowering in the tree because of the same huge dog she had so calmly ignored. It was also the same dog which had slobbered friendliness all over me when I had reached the ground.

Two more sips of tea, and Stonewall spoke again. "You all had questions about Moth-Wallet Bugsby."

I spoke. "We noticed in a history book that your father was his business partner."

He twisted his face to express distaste. His wrinkles were as deep as Old Lady Bugsby's, but unlike her wrinkles, his were set in grooves from years of smiling, not frowning.

"You could say that," he said. "He lent my father money once."

We waited.

"You want me to continue," he finally said. "But I'm not sure I will. Seventy-five years ago, the entire situation was a shameful secret to our family. Some things don't change."

Stonewall laughed. "Seventy-five years is a long time. I was around when trains were faster than planes. In fact, I'm about that old myself and ask me if *that* feels old."

"Does that—oooof!" Lisa elbowed Ralphy before he could finish.

"Mr. Sawyer," I said. "Please let me explain why we're asking. Then maybe you can decide what to tell us."

I told him about the map and the rumored treasure and how everybody in town was after it.

He listened without moving. Because of his dark glasses and the stillness of his face, it was hard to decide what he was thinking. When I finished, he reached gingerly for the small table beside him, and set down his empty cup. "You're hoping, I suppose, I can give you clues as to its location."

"Yes, sir."

He steepled his fingers underneath his chin. "If everything else is already public knowledge, I can easily find out what *you* know. Why shouldn't I keep *my* information and discover the gold myself?" He smiled lightly to take any offense out of his question.

I hadn't thought of that.

"As you can see"—he spread his hands at the bareness of the room—"there's not much left of the Sawyer fortune. Maybe I could use the money in my declining years."

None of us had an answer. Ticking of a clock somewhere else in the house grew louder in the new silence.

"Read me what you have," he said abruptly.

On a photocopied piece of paper, I had the information from the fifth chapter of one of Jamesville's more recent history books. I cleared my throat. "Much of Jamesville's economic activity at the turn of the century—"

Stonewall put up an arm. "Ricky, if you don't mind, will you let Lisa read? Her voice brings back so many nice memories."

Lisa smiled and took the page from me. "Much of Jamesville's economic activity at the turn of the century consisted of a network of businesses begun by Jonathan Sawyer. At one point, his wealth was estimated to be so great that he could have purchased every property in the small but growing town. Few denied he was the richest man in the county."

"Father, Father, Father," Stonewall whispered to himself.

Lisa waited respectfully before beginning again. "Misfortune, however, in the form of a simple but devastating health problem cost Sawyer dearly at the peak of his wealth. For three years, he and his family suffered from a persistent form of stomach illness, which in terms of modern medicine would be diagnosed as dysentery. Most Jamesville old-timers recall that the constant weakening effects of dysentery's stomach cramping and diarrhea robbed Jonathan Sawyer of his legendary energy. By the time he regained good health, his business empire was on the verge of toppling.

"In 1917, after a year of illness, Sawyer joined forces with local business rival Frederick Bugsby, and in so doing, managed to preserve the manufacturing companies that were so vital to the Jamesville economy. Five years later, Bugsby bought out his partner, and from there developed the original network of businesses without any influence from Jonathan Sawyer. In the following years—"

"That's fine," Stonewall said quietly. "I'm sure there are few references to the Sawyer family after that."

Our silence was enough of a reply for him.

"Those years of illness certainly did my father in," Stonewall mused. "I was born halfway through—blind because my mother was ill too—so I don't remember it, but my brothers and sisters told me about it often enough. All of them were constantly sick. Father and Mother could barely keep the household going, let alone devote time to business. Folks said it was the Devil's work. That anyone as rich as my father must have a secret crime, and justice was finally being served. The worst of it was not knowing if it would hit again. They could be fine for a month, even two, and from nowhere, it would hit again. The fear of not knowing nearly destroyed our family."

Ralphy, our walking encyclopedia, hicked and nodded vigorously. "Doctors today say that the dysentery bug can stay in your system for years and—"

"Ralphy," Lisa said gently, "I'm sure Mr. Sawyer knows all about it."

"Sorry."

Stonewall leaned back in his chair. "First of all, is the light on? I know this time of year it gets dark early and of course I don't need it . . . "

"It's on," Lisa said. "And you're very nice for worrying."

He shook his head in admiration of her gentleness. "How could I possibly refuse to help a girl like you?" He slapped his hands together as if coming to a sudden decision. "This is the deal. I'll tell you as much as I can. But I want your help keeping everyone else away. At my age, I don't like being disturbed much and if *you've* decided I've got information, it won't take the rest of town long to decide the same thing. How does that sound?"

"Great!" all of us said at once.

"Not so fast. It's getting late, and we're nearly done for the day. Tomorrow, come back after school. The first thing on the agenda is a little painting. Then we'll talk."

Mike's eyes opened wide and he silently mouthed a question in my direction. *PAINTING?* I shrugged at him.

"Are you bringing Joel?" Stonewall asked.

I coughed. "He . . . um . . . somehow manages to . . . uh . . . follow us no matter what we try."

Stonewall nodded. "Just wanted to prepare myself. My heart hasn't had that much action in a decade."

Joel smiled at the attention. He pulled his hand free from mine and approached Stonewall.

"Mister," he said, "can you make more of that music talk to me?"

I coughed again. "Joel, the nice man doesn't make the music. He plays it from the stereo." I stopped. "Mr. Sawyer, I *did* want to ask you about the compact disc you played while we sat in your tree."

"It's called 'blues,' Ricky. I don't imagine you hear it on your radio station much." Stonewall smiled at me as he spoke, then leaned forward and whispered in Joel's ear. Joel trotted to the porch and returned with something he held carefully in both arms.

"An alto saxophone," Lisa exclaimed with delight. "Not a CD."

"You played the music yourself?" Mike asked. "Cooler than the coolest."

A sad smile from Stonewall. "Thank you, son. Trouble is, when a man plays the blues so that you hear his soul, it's generally because he's had the blues once or twice himself."

He wet the reed of the mouthpiece by gently putting it between his lips. He blew once experimentally to catch the tone.

Then Stonewall took a breath. "Here you are, little one. Let's see if this talks to you again."

Clear and sweet, the music filled inside me an ache I hadn't known was there until those notes began their slow and rising cry.

Stonewall played with total concentration. He poured a softness out of the saxophone that I sensed verged on genius, a softness that seemed wrong to interrupt with any good-byes.

So we listened as long as we could, then left the house silently in the beginning dusk, followed down the street by those lonely lonely blues.

14

Nobody, of course, mentioned I would solve the mystery of the treasure map that night. Even if someone had, the way conversation went, I still might not have left the supper table in a big hurry.

Dad sputtered on his coffee. "Stonewall Sawyer? Stonewall Sawyer played you guys some blues?!? In person?!?"

I looked at him strangely. "Sure, Dad. Joel asked if he would make the music talk again and he played for all of us in his front room."

Dad's coffee mug was still halfway to his mouth, frozen in the same position it had been when I had mentioned Stonewall's name.

"Come on," he pleaded. "You're kidding me, right? Stonewall didn't really just sit down and play for you."

I nodded again. "Yes, Dad. I asked him what he called that kind of music, and he said 'blues' and then got Joel to get his saxophone."

Dad moaned. "I can't believe it. Stonewall Sawyer hasn't been public in ten years, and his first audience is a bunch of kids who don't even know him or what he's playing." He turned to Mom and extended his moan. "Stephanie, can you bring me a towel for these tears?"

Mom patted his hand. "There, there, honey. Big boys don't cry."

It was fun, watching Dad in agony. "So this guy's good?" I asked as stupidly as possible, just to rub it in.

Dad set his cup down, then placed his arms on the table, buried his head between them, and moaned louder.

Mom stifled a giggle.

"Good?" came Dad's muffled voice. "Good? Was Babe Ruth a good ball player? Is it a long way to the moon? The guy's a legend."

"Ricky," Mom explained, "you probably haven't heard much about Stonewall. He moved back here just after you were born. He's been so reclusive, folks just stopped talking about him."

Dad faked a sob, then sat up again.

"I'm OK now," he sniffed. "I'll get over this."

"Seriously, Dad."

"Seriously? I'd give a week's wages for the privilege of listening to that man. His real name's Ernie, you know. He got the name Stonewall because one day another legend named Louis Armstrong heard him play. Louis said . . ." Dad dropped his voice deep and gravelly, " 'That man plays sax so good even the stone walls be meltin' to listen.' "

Mom said unnecessarily, "Your father knows a lot about Stonewall's career."

I closed my eyes and re-listened to those sweet rising notes. "I knew he was good, Dad, even without knowing about him."

"Hope for my boy yet," Dad breathed.

I ignored him. "The stuff he was playing made me goose-pimply sad. But a good sad. It's hard to explain."

Mom got up. "Sorry, I need to get ready for a meeting tonight."

Dad leaned back and sipped on his coffee. He was so lost in thought, he didn't even notice Mom leave.

"That's why blues are my favorite," he said as he turned his cup in his hand. "It's a good kind of sad. Just like life."

I shook my head. "How can you say life is sad? Lots of people have love and families and stuff like that."

Dad replied with a smile that was gentle and small. A realization brushed me. He wasn't just *Dad*, he was a person just like me, who maybe had dreams that didn't work out, or things to be scared of.

"Son, as time passes, everything must eventually change. Understand? No matter how good something might be, some day it'll go. That's why life is sad. For example, your mother and I love each other dearly and it's very good. But some day, she'll go, or I'll go, and the one left alone will be very sad. The funny thing is, the better something is now, the sadder you become when it's gone."

I heard Stonewall's music in my head, and began to understand it more. Then I felt some anger. "If everything's going to fall apart in life anyway, why care? Why start anything good?"

His laugh matched the quietness of his smile. "That's what's noble about being human. Out of all the creatures in this world, we're the ones who understand that someday we'll die, that someday the love we let grow will cause us pain. And—this is the noble part—despite knowing that, we love and live as best we can."

"Great," I said, not meaning it. "I can hardly wait until I'm grown-up enough for that kind of hurt."

This time Dad grinned ear to ear. "You're forgetting something. God. He is the Unchangeable. With Him, the love we create is permanent. Without Him, everything is nothing. Stonewall— one of the best blues players alive—will tell you the same thing, son. As God's creature, love and live as best you can, because loving and living is glorious. When life is finished, and you're with God, you'll truly understand what it was all about."

Once more, the music in my head. I grinned back. "So that's what blues are all about. God."

"When you believe in God, you see Him everywhere."

Before I could think that through, Mom reappeared.

"Has your father finished his theory on sadness?"

"Yes, dear," he said.

Mom shook her head. "The first time he told it to me, I cried on his shoulder. Because by then it was too late. I already loved the turkey."

"That was happiness making you cry," Dad protested. "Because that was also the night I asked you to marry me. Remember? All that moonlight and my very first Buick and we held hands and—"

Mother coughed and changed the subject. "I'm here to ask your oldest son if he knows anything about my hand mirror. There's no way I can check the back of my hair without it."

Hand mirror. Hand mirror. Why did it jog my memory?

I snapped my fingers. "Joel had it last. We were trying a peanut butter and chocolate hiccup cure and ... and I bet Joel left it in my room or his. I'll get it now."

I darted upstairs thinking I'd come right back and ask Dad more questions about Stonewall and the Sawyer family. Or so I thought, especially when I found the hand mirror so quickly.

It was under Joel's bed. No surprise there.

But my treasure map was on the floor, instead of safely in the drawer of my night table. Major surprise. I sucked in a lungful of air to yell outrage, but as I picked up the mirror in one hand, I noticed something in reflection and I forgot to breathe.

The map in my other hand showed clearly in the mirror. And it dawned on me that it showed *very* clearly.

I brought the mirror closer to the map.

My lungful of air did not go to waste.

"Yahoooo!" I shouted. "We're going to be zillionaires!"

15

Grown-ups sometimes have no sense of perspective. Here we were, on the verge of discovering more gold than you could carry in a wheelbarrow—or at least close to that amount—and they had the nerve to decide a good night's sleep was more important.

As if I could sleep anyway.

I stared at the ceiling. *Would Mrs. Reynolds make me keep my promise about buying her a convertible? It probably wouldn't matter. There'd be enough money to buy ten convertibles. No, twenty.*

I tossed to the other side of the bed, stuck my head over the edge of my bed, and stared at the floor. All I needed to find that fortune was daylight, the help of my friends, and one final breakthrough.

Getting daylight would be no problem. It was less than twelve hours away. Of course, the way time was going, that felt like twelve centuries. Still, I'd be surprised if it didn't arrive on schedule.

I'd be just as surprised if the help of my friends didn't arrive at the same time. I'd already called Mike and Ralphy and Lisa with the news. We were going to meet before school began.

That only left one small snag. The final breakthrough.

Sure, the map was clear to read in mirrored reverse. Sure, some of the crooked lines matched some Jamesville streets. Sure, the city hall was marked in the right place. But what was that weird curving line through everything? And what about the big upside-down box drawn overtop the map? The one that seemed irritably familiar?

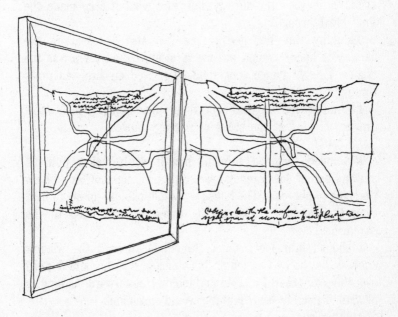

, I ran the map's words through my head for the nine-hundredth time. *Gold shall be the reward to the one who searches deep and hard.* That meant it was buried. *Yet start through the soot for the discovery of the loot.* OK, it was buried in a fireplace. *Things beneath the surface of sight provide a treasure to the one who sees it right.* Yeah, yeah, we know it's buried. But where?

I sighed into the darkness.

Without the breakthrough, we were no farther ahead. And how long before Squinty Eyes or Yellow Fingers discovered the mirror trick?

I giggled to myself. Probably never. Those two guys didn't know what combs were for.

But the other people in town. Someone else might realize it soon. Or maybe they already had. And what if *they* made the final breakthrough?

Thinking was not getting me far. Maybe rereading the Jamesville history would put me to sleep. If not, there was the chance I might notice something I'd missed my first ten times through.

I found my reading flashlight, then pulled open my night table drawer, wincing at the creak of squeaky hinges.

No book!

My fingers twitched, thinking how it would feel to pull the stuffing out of Joel's teddy bear. I shut my light off and began tiptoeing to his room. The house was quiet enough for me to hear even the random clicks of the furnace vents deep in the basement.

I slipped into Joel's room. Streetlight through the window showed that he was asleep on his stomach with his arm flopped over the teddy bear. I relaxed and took a step forward. As long as he had his teddy bear, nothing would wake him.

Another step and—

"Gggnnnnhhhh!" I bit back a scream and forced it to echo in my stomach. One tear managed to trickle from the side of my eye. *Why did that dumb kid brother of mine need to leave a toy train where any sane person knew it would be stepped on?*

When my urge to howl subsided, I moved to his bed and felt underneath for the history book. That's where it had to be. Near where I had found the treasure map.

"Gggnnnnhhhh!" Another scream reached my stomach instead

of yelping out my lungs. I reached underneath with my other
hand and pulled the tip of a dart that had imbedded itself
between my thumb and thumbnail.

Finally, my hand bumped against a large book.

I relaxed, safe.

"Gggnnnnhhhh!" Halfway under a bed with both arms extended is not a good position to be in when the person who is
supposed to be sleeping above you decides to hop out of bed.

"I'm going to the bathroom," Joel explained as if it was natu-
ral to use an older brother as a rug.

"Wonderful," I grunted straight into the floor.

He didn't even step on his train.

* * * * * * * *

Train. Train. Train.

A thought surged through me with enough power to shoot me
straight up in bed at 3 A.M.

What was it about trains?

I had been dreaming trains—old-fashioned history book
trains—ever since falling into a restless sleep. *What was
bumping so hard against my subconscious?*

I took a deep breath and slowly reviewed anything train related from the previous few days.

Hadn't Stonewall Sawyer said something about trains?

Yes! He'd told us he was eighty-two. *What were his exact
words?* "I was around when trains were faster than planes."

I closed my eyes to picture the slower trains. I saw in my mind
exactly what I had been dreaming. An old-fashioned locomotive,
just like the one in the Jamesville history book, chugging around
a corner with a cloud of black rising from its smokestack. *Why
did that seem so import—*

It hit me.

Soot. I let my breath out slowly. That was it. Soot. *Yet start through the soot for the discovery of the loot.*

Moth-Wallet Bugsby hadn't meant soot from a fireplace. No. He'd been thinking trains the way he knew them most of his adult life. Trains that blew sooty black smoke.

I was nearly there. I could feel it. *But what was left?*

I found my flashlight, clicked it on, and flipped through the trusty Jamesville history book. Where was that picture of the train?

On page 144, I found the answer to everything.

The photograph that dominated the page showed the locomotive emerging from underneath a bridge. Behind the bridge, the rail cars formed a long line that disappeared around a bend. Two things made me certain I had discovered the location of his treasure.

The first was the black smoke pouring up into the curved underpart of the bridge. No doubt the structure would have been greasy with soot — *the soot that hid the loot.*

And the second was the shape of the bridge. It formed an upside-down box that roughly matched the shape of the one superimposed upon the treasure map.

Both things meant that the curved line running through the map must be the tracks. Where the curved line entered the map, there was the narrow valley of Lumber Creek. The tracks still existed there, but farther down the line, halfway into Jamesville, they had been redirected. Obviously, that had happened after Moth-Wallet had drawn his map and that, of course, explained why it hadn't made immediate sense.

Everything fit. The treasure was ours.

I grinned at the ceiling with satisfaction. When sunshine woke me, the grin was still there.

16

Holding a paintbrush was not my idea of searching for treasure.

"How do you spell *quarantined?*" I mumbled to Lisa. She stood beside me, holding a wood panel upright on Stonewall Sawyer's scraggly front lawn.

"You once told me that guys knew everything."

"Only everything important. How to spell *quarantine* is not on my list of important."

"By the frown on your face, I'd say it seems important now."

Never argue with a woman. "OK. It's important. I confess. Guys don't quite know everything. Just tell me."

"It starts with a 'Q.' And that's always followed by a 'U.' "

"Lisa! We don't have time for this."

"Q-U-A-R-A-N-T-I-N-E-D." She smiled prettily.

I managed to grumble despite her smile. "I don't mind doing this. Not at all. But we could be faster about it. After all, Ralphy and Mike are waiting for us."

"Another five minutes won't matter."

She was right, of course. Stonewall Sawyer had been nice enough to offer his help the afternoon before. Even if we didn't need it anymore, we still owed him the courtesy of fulfilling our part of the bargain.

I finished painting the rest of the letters. QUARANTINED DUE
TO POSSIBLE DYSENTERY. As Stonewall had pointed out, *possible* only meant maybe, and *maybe* also meant maybe not, so
the sign didn't really lie. And it would certainly keep visitors
away, especially ones who had read about his family's mysterious
illness in a history book.

As I hammered the nail to attach it to the same tree we had
used for yesterday's panic retreat from Blue, Stonewall called
from his rocking chair on the porch.

"Sounds like a completed job to me. Why don't you both come
up here and ask the questions you had in mind."

I followed Lisa to the porch. Both of us stepped around Blue,
who filled most of the sidewalk in front of the house.

"Stonewall," she started.

"You've changed your mind about questions," he announced.

Lisa's eyes widened. It was good to see her caught off guard
for a change.

"How did you know?"

He grinned. "First, no hiccups. That tells me no Ralphy. Also
no Mike. Second, the tone of your voice. Hesitant and slightly
worried."

Lisa blushed. "Ricky and I both want to spend time asking
questions. But different questions than we had planned. And
maybe tomorrow or the day after."

Stonewall nodded patiently as he continued rocking. "So,
Ricky, you think you know where the treasure is."

My turn to be floored. "Yes, but—"

"That was easy to figure out too. At this stage, nothing—I
would bet—could tear you guys away from your treasure hunt."

He paused and rocked, then held up a hand. "The only thing
that puzzles me is why you stopped here to paint that sign. You
don't have the treasure yet and you have a place to search; why
waste time?"

"We want to be friends," Lisa said simply.

The chair stopped rocking. Blue twitched once in his sleep. Lisa and I waited.

Stonewall said nothing until he resumed rocking. "Friends. I like the sound of that. A lot." Then he pointed away from the house. "Now get. Find your fortune. And come back later and tell me all about it."

* * * * * * * *

We stood in the center of the bridge just outside the far side of Jamesville.

"You took long enough," Mike said. "We've barely got an hour of bright sunlight left."

I leaned forward, hands on my knees, and glared upward at him as I gasped air into my burning lungs. Lisa had been right. Killing myself to get there a few minutes early didn't make any difference.

"If he could *HIC* speak, he'd probably remind you who solved the map part," Ralphy said to Mike while he uncoiled a length of rope from his shoulders.

Lisa arrived on her bicycle just as I had enough energy to lean my own bike against the bridge railing. She noted my exhaustion, but wisely decided against reminding me she had been right about not rushing here. "So this is it," she remarked calmly.

This was it. The only bridge in or near Jamesville old enough to qualify as the one in the picture. It crossed Lumber Creek's narrow valley; the tracks and the valley followed the path of the creek into town.

Behind us, the tracks curved out of sight. Ahead, the tracks continued in a straight line directly to Jamesville.

By looking at the grass pushing its way up through buckled pavement, I guessed the one-lane road leading to the bridge had been abandoned for years. Now, the bridge and lane were simply a convenient footpath for the people who lived here on the outskirts of town.

That suited us just fine. We appreciated the privacy.

Mike rubbed his hands. "Me and The Hiccup Kid—" Ralphy fought his next hiccup without success and then turned red at his nickname —"will tie the rope and make sure it stays secure. We'll pull you up when you find the map."

I nodded.

"What about trains?" Lisa asked.

"They're big and have cabooses," I said.

She shook her hair impatiently. "Nitwit. I mean what about if one comes."

"Women don't know much important stuff, do they? You can hear a train horn miles away. It'll give us lots of time."

She shrugged.

By then, Ralphy and Mike had the rope ready. They threw it over the side. Its bottom end almost reached the tracks. I was so pumped with adrenaline that I barely noticed the climb down.

Once I was below the suspension beams, I swung gently in to look upward.

"See anything?" Mike shouted.

"Not yet. It's dark."

"Use your flashlight."

"Thanks for the brainstorm, Mike."

Except there was a slight problem. I wasn't strong enough to hold on with one hand and get my flashlight with the other.

"Pull me up for a second, all right?"

They did and I explained my problem.

"I'll climb down to the tracks and shine it for you," Mike said.

"Hey. I'm part of this too," Lisa interrupted. "You guys are rope pullers. You can let me be a light shiner."

Mike shrugged.

This time, Lisa went down the rope first. She waited on the

tracks for me, and as I swung in, she beamed the light upwards.

"I can't see anything yet," I grunted. "But there's not much room to hide anything."

Four more swinging passes underneath the bridge showed just as little as the first two.

"Ricky!" Lisa shouted.

I was looking so hard, I barely heard her.

"What?" This hard work was not putting me in a good mood.

"It's a train!"

Then I remembered what I should have remembered much earlier. Trains only blast their horns at intersections. And there were none for miles before this bridge. With the curve so near, the wind so high, and us concentrating on the map, we hadn't noticed it until its headlights rounded the bend.

I scanned down the track.

There was no way for Lisa to run ahead far enough in time to escape it!

She knew it too. She was already scrambling up the rope.

I began to pull myself up.

"Ricky! I'm slipping."

I didn't have to look to know how little time remained. The approaching roar of the engine and the painful brightness of the headlights and the frantic blaring of the warning horn told me I couldn't even pause to think.

I slipped down the rope toward Lisa and somehow found the strength to hold the rope with one hand and extend the other down to her.

"Climb over me!" I shouted above the roar.

She hesitated.

"Now!" I screamed.

They say that people can jump ten-foot-high fences when a bull is chasing them. I believe it. Earlier, I had not been able to reach for a flashlight with my free hand. Now, the rush of tons of steel was enough to give me strength I didn't believe possible. In one sudden motion, I yanked her up high enough to let her grab the rope above my head. She pushed off my shoulders and reached girder height.

Safe!

And I knew I wouldn't make it.

Her push had sent me — and the rope — out from the bridge. It swung back directly at the locomotive.

I had one, small chance. I let go.

The headlights etched the outline of the girder so clearly that I felt as if I were in slow motion. My fingertips caught the edge and with a final shout of terror I pulled myself up.

I blinked, and the headlights and blaring horn passed beneath me. A howling fury of noise threatened to shake me loose from the girder, but with the last of my strength I wrapped myself tight to the cold iron that had saved my life.

The shaking and roaring lasted longer than my worst nightmare until finally the caboose passed beneath me in a blur of red. A dying clackety-clack of iron wheels on steel tracks replaced the numbing roar in my head. The shaking of the bridge slowed, then stopped.

For a moment, all I could do was silently pray "thank You" again and again. I wasn't worried that God might not hear. If He had been close enough for this miracle, He was close enough to know each of my thoughts.

I finally realized someone was calling.

"Ricky! Ricky! Tell us you're alive!" came the shout from above.

I looked sideways and saw the rope swaying. Empty.

It took a few seconds to swallow away the dryness of my mouth and throat. Then I struggled to find something to say. After all, it isn't too often you get to be a hero by surviving your own stupidity.

"Ricky! Ricky!" The shouts became more frantic.

I remembered a quote by Mark Twain, the author of *Tom Sawyer*, when newspapers published a story about his death.

I reached out and tugged on the rope, then began climbing back up to the bridge.

"The rumors of my death," I began bravely when I reached the top and collapsed onto the surface of the bridge, "have been greatly exaggerated." Then, despite my best efforts to be cool, I fainted.

I later heard again the sounds of the wind through the crackling autumn leaves, and I began to speak.

"When I open my eyes," I announced calmly, "that had better be Lisa who was applying mouth-to-mouth resuscitation. Because if it's Mike, I'll have to gargle for a month."

I opened my eyes. Lisa's cheeks were red from embarrassment. Which relieved me greatly.

"Good to *HIC* see you," Ralphy said over her shoulder. *If he had been under the bridge, there would be no way he'd still have the hiccups.*

Lisa quickly stood.

Ralphy and Mike helped me back to my feet. Joel was there too. No surprise.

"I've been following people," he announced.

No surprise there. I waved him into silence. Which, naturally, was a mistake. Joel talks so rarely, a person should examine every word closely.

"No map," Mike said. "But at least we have you."

I shook my head slowly. "This was the only place possible as shown by that map," I told them grimly. "I don't know where to look next."

Mike scuffed his feet on the ground. "Me neither."

"Unless," I paused as I reached behind me, "unless I check the back of my shirt."

I pulled out a flat package wrapped in well-worn and oiled black leather. "What could *this* be?"

Mike howled in delight.

Ralphy's hiccupping tripled in excitement.

Lisa smiled.

"Found it on the girder. It was taped flat and painted black to match the color of the iron," I told them. I didn't mention I'd squashed my face against it in terror and had barely enough strength left in my arms to pull it free before tugging on the rope for my final upward climb. "Now all we have to do is open it and discover where the gold is buried."

With a dramatic flourish, I presented it to Mike.

"Not so fast," a gruff voice said from behind us before he could take it.

We all whirled at once.

Squinty Eyes and Yellow Fingers!

"That's them," Joel announced. "I followed them here."

Wonderful time for a sudden news flash.

Squinty Eyes continued. "Anything in that package that belonged to Moth-Wallet Bugsby is now the property of his only heir, Ethel Bugsby."

"Yeah," Yellow Fingers smirked. "After that wild goose chase you sent us on in the library, we decided to join forces with Miss Bugsby. Which is why she hired us to follow you dumb puppies all over town. Miss Bugsby and the police'll be here shortly to make sure that everything is done legal like."

He dug into his coat and found a cigarette. After lighting it and taking a deep drag, he flopped his nicotine-stained fingers in my direction.

"So hand it over, bud."

17

"Small consolation," Mayor Thorpe said as he placed a hand on my shoulder, "but 'most everybody in town thinks Ethel Bugsby pulled a rotten stunt on you guys."

"It'd be nice if a person could deposit consolation in the bank, sir." It was only Saturday morning, but enough people had said the same thing over the last few days so that if putting it in the bank was possible, we'd be millionaires.

"Good one, son." He shook his head in sympathy. "Well, time for my civic duty." Mayor Thorpe pushed on, artfully maneuvering his big belly in front of him as he moved through the tightly jammed people who formed the crowd in front of the library.

"I can't bear to watch," Mike moaned.

Bear! Where was Joel?

In the distraction of jostling for position, I'd absent-mindedly given him back his teddy bear. He could be anywhere.

I tried looking past Mike's shoulder, then around Lisa and Ralphy. All I saw were legs and arms and shoulders of the grown-ups milling in front of us.

Then I realized I didn't care. Losing Moth-Wallet Bugsby's buried trunk—the one that now sat on display in front of the crowd and that was so big it had taken three grown men to carry

87

it—was so depressing that Joel could cause a stampede and it wouldn't matter how much of the blame I got.

The expressions on the faces of Mike and Lisa matched mine. So did Ralphy's except before, during, or after a hiccup. We didn't want to be here, yet we couldn't stay away.

It was a simple reason.

The trunk had not been opened. At all.

Securely locked, it stood up there behind the microphone in musty glory, tantalizing the entire public gathering. Alongside Deputy Mayor Higgins, Ethel Bugsby glowered proudly beside it, dressed again in starched black from neck to toes. Behind her, Squinty Eyes and Yellow Fingers, both with uncombed hair and in frayed suits, trying to enjoy the respectability of being part of the proceedings.

Mayor Thorpe stepped beside them and cleared his throat into the microphone until everyone became silent. He pulled a paper from his pocket.

"Fourscore and seven years ago, our forefathers . . . oh, wrong speech."

Then he grinned to show he was joking, but most everyone in Jamesville had heard him try that one before, so few people laughed.

He cleared his throat again and peered at the paper.

"As you all know," he began, "Fred Bugsby was one of Jamesville's most upstanding citizens for many decades. He was kind, generous, well-loved, intelligent, very handsome, good with children, concerned about all human beings and . . . and . . . and . . . "

He stopped and looked up at Old Lady Bugsby in irritation. "Oh for pete's sake, Ethel, your handwriting is impossible to read."

Mayor Thorpe folded the paper and handed it to Ethel Bugsby. She frowned, but he waved away her protest before it could begin. Then he squarely faced the crowd.

"OK, it's like this. All of you know a few weeks ago we began to dedicate a statue to Fred Bugsby in this very same spot. So you've already heard the speech stuff about the man."

He leaned forward. "What's that, Mr. McKinnley?" He shook his head in irritation. "My secretary's told you a dozen times. It was kids, not Germans. Watermelon, not a bomb. And the town is *not* going to pay for the dry cleaning of your suit."

Mayor Thorpe's sigh whistled through the microphone. "Anyway, last Tuesday, those kids redeemed themselves by brilliantly solving the puzzle of a long buried treasure and . . . "

He waved away the grumbles of Squinty Eyes and Yellow Fingers ". . . and other citizens were able to take advantage of it through legal procedures. As a result, we have before us Moth-Wall—" he coughed furiously "—Fred Bugsby's legendary fortune."

Mayor Thorpe paused and swept his arm in the direction of the trunk. "And, as most of you know, the second map that led to its discovery in the center of the town park had a conditional request plainly printed upon it."

This time, all of the people around us sighed. I knew exactly what they were all thinking. In going through the park, they had all walked past the treasure hundreds of times in their lifetimes, not knowing it was buried a few feet beneath them.

"That request was that the trunk be opened at a public gathering. The promise was that if it was so done, Fred Bugsby would see that all who viewed its contents would be rewarded. Ethel Bugsby, of course, did not dream for a moment of doing otherwise once she saw the request."

Of course, I thought sourly, *she didn't have much choice since our chief of police had been another witness right beside her while she smugly unfurled the treasure map in front of us on the bridge last Tuesday.*

"So here we are," Mayor Thorpe concluded. "Ready to open a trunk that has been securely shut for decades."

He stepped aside as Yellow Fingers and Squinty Eyes elbowed each other to get to the trunk first. Yellow Fingers held the hammer. Squinty Eyes held the chisel.

Squinty Eyes stepped on the feet of Yellow Fingers, managed to reach the trunk first, and then bowed grandly. Yellow Fingers, the loser of their brief tussle, gave him a dirty look from behind.

Squinty Eyes bowed—trying for applause—then shrugged at the silence before placing his chisel against the lock.

Yellow Fingers was still upset. He swung his hammer, and missed the chisel but not the hand holding it. He grinned as Squinty Eyes jumped and howled in pain. *That* drew applause.

Ethel Bugsby stamped her feet in anger, walked up to Yellow Fingers, and pulled on his ear until he dropped the hammer.

She hissed the crowd into silence, and furiously smashed the hammer against the lock until it broke off. The clattering of old iron falling to the platform seemed magnified as everyone held their breath in anticipation.

"Finally," Old Lady Bugsby crowed as she straightened her tall, scrawny body, "the last of my father's fortune!"

She paused for a moment to add tension.

The flag above us flapped in the wind, then stopped. It seemed the crystal silence would last forever as we all strained to see. Until Ralphy hiccuped loudly.

That broke the tension. "Come on, Ethel," someone called. "Spare us the melodramatics!"

She hmmpphed loudly, then reached down to pull on the lid.

Mayor Thorpe, Deputy Mayor Higgins, Yellow Fingers, and Squinty Eyes—who was sucking his thumb in agony—all leaned forward.

Just before she could yank it open, Joel wandered to the front. He set his teddy bear down beside the trunk.

In the quietness of anticipation, every word of his reached us far too clearly.

"Hi. Are you Miss Skinflint Scrooge?" he asked with charming innocence.

I groaned inside, knowing all the grown-ups in my household wouldn't take long to figure out where he'd heard that from.

"Skinflint Scrooge!"

Joel surveyed the trunk, then patted it. "You're a nice lady to open this for my brother. Want me to help?"

Old Lady Bugsby ground her teeth, a sound that carried into the microphone and through the speakers. Then she picked up his teddy bear and jammed it back into his arms.

"Git," she hissed.

I was given no time to worry about how much trouble my kid brother had just earned me. He tucked the teddy bear under his shirt and spun around. As he disappeared into the crowd, Old Lady Bugsby yanked open the lid of the trunk.

There was a loud crackle and a SNAP!

Smoke billowed outward from the trunk. Old Lady Bugsby threw up her arms and fell backward. But it was too late.

Before the hem of her dress touched the ground, a horrendous KA-BOOM thundered across the crowd and drowned out the screams of panic. A geyser of darkness exploded outward in a deadly dense cloud!

Many things happened as a result of that explosion.

Mayor Thorpe landed on Deputy Mayor Higgins, which cracked two ribs for each of them, but Deputy Mayor Higgins counted himself lucky because Mayor Thorpe's broad back became the perfect umbrella against the rest of what happened in the next second and a half.

Gossip says that no matter what they try at the beauty shop, probably nothing will ever turn Old Lady Bugsby's silver hair back to silver.

And Mr. McKinnley remained in his house for the next three months, only using the telephone to call Mayor Thorpe's secretary and shout abuse about his new dry cleaning bill and the lack of protection this town provided from invading armies.

Everybody else at the front of the crowd walked through town afterward for days with purple-masklike faces and terribly stained hands.

That, however, was the aftermath of the explosion. The explosion itself mushroomed so violently, it threw the entire crowd to the ground in panic.

Then, as people began to realize they weren't hurt, they struggled to their feet again. And one inescapable fact slowly dawned upon them as they searched each other's faces for signs of damage.

Moth-Wallet Bugsby had booby-trapped the trunk.

Measurements taken later showed that the tank inside it had contained fifty-five gallons of newspaper ink before becoming Jamesville's practical joke of the century.

"A purple tongue! In all my years I've never heard of such a thing."

"Yes, sir," I said. "You should *see* it . . . " As I realized what I was saying to Stonewall Sawyer, I stopped and mentally kicked myself for being so stupid.

It didn't dim his wide grin in the least. "Come on, son. I've been blind a long time. You don't have to worry about my feelings. Tell me about Joel's tongue."

Joel looked up from where he was scratching between Blue's ears. His face was still a raccoon mask of dark ink. He stuck his tongue out at me. Most of *that* purple had faded by now. The four of us—Stonewall in his rocking chair, Joel, Blue, and I—filled the front porch of his tiny house. Louis Armstrong music—light jazz this time—softly drifted out from Stonewall's stereo.

"Well," I began again, "it happened three days ago, Saturday, when Old Lady Bugsby opened her father's trunk. I'm sure you heard about *that.*"

Stonewall chuckled. "It figures the old miser wouldn't share anything except trouble. Even long dead."

"Joel was at the front of the crowd," I explained. "He'd stopped to turn around, and just as he was sticking his tongue out at the mean lady—Old Lady Bugsby of course—all that ink exploded from the trunk."

Stonewall shook his head and chuckled more. "That's a pretty good story. Something you'll want to save for the day when you become a writer."

"Yes, sir."

"Notice I said *when,* not *if,*" Stonewall said. "That's the thing about dreaming. If you keep trying and never give up, and if you practice at it, you can become most anything you dream. It's what I learned from music. I made the big time on desire and discipline. Not talent."

As I tried absorbing that, his tone shifted and became almost businesslike. "What else was in the trunk?"

Lisa stuck her head onto the porch from his front room "Tea's almost ready."

Stonewall smiled as she went back to the kitchen, then repeated his question. "Anything else in the trunk?"

"Only some junk. I called them old-fashioned pots and pans until Ralphy corrected me. Not that any of us care about a make-believe treasure anymore."

"He still hiccuping?"

"Yup. In fact, he's at the doctor's office right now. Mike's with him for moral support. In case a needle appears."

Stonewall nodded, then listened and hummed to a few bars of the music.

Lisa walked out with a tray holding a teapot, cups and saucers, and a bowl of cookies. She insisted on pouring for all of us, and then settled in a wicker chair beside me.

A few minutes of friendly music listening passed.

"Junk you say." Stonewall was leaning forward again.

"Junk? Oh, in the trunk. Ralphy explained they were containers a pharmacist might use. Kind of a silver-gray crockery. He said some was clay and enamel. Some was made of pewter."

Stonewall stopped leaning and started rocking. "Yup. Pewter. It's a mixture of silver and lead. Ralphy sounds like a knowledgeable young man."

"The computer genius type," Lisa said. "Knows lots of encyclopedia trivia and that kind of stuff."

More slow rocking. Stonewall finished his tea. I took the cup from him and set it back on the tray.

"Let me tell you guys something about growing old," Stonewall said. "When you're old, you start to think about being gone and how that's it for you on earth. And you wonder what you'll have left behind to show for all that time."

Joel scratched between Blue's huge ears a little harder, and the dog thumped his tail in gratitude. Stonewall stopped long enough to smile at the interruption, then continued.

"It drives some people crazy," he said. "To grow old and suddenly realize that when they're gone, they'll probably be forgotten soon enough."

It was interesting to listen, but I couldn't figure why he had switched subjects so abruptly from Moth-Wallet Bugsby's trunk.

"In my case," he said, "I feel peaceful about the process. I've had a good life, and my faith in God lets me know when I move on, it'll be to a better place. And, of course, there's always my music. When I'm gone, the recordings will remind people that old Stonewall took a pretty good swipe at living."

He ran his hand through his short, bristly hair. "So, ex-treasure hunters, why am I telling you both this?"

Lisa poured another cup of tea and placed it back in Stonewall's hands. "I'll guess," she said as she sat back down. "Fred Bugsby was afraid of dying?"

"Something like that. Which also means I think you shouldn't give up on that treasure of his."

He said it with such authority that electricity shot through me.

This time it was my turn to lean forward in sudden interest. "I'm sorry, sir, I missed that connection."

Stonewall sipped on his tea and kept us in suspense. Then he said, "It touched me very much that you helped me with that sign when you thought the treasure hunt was over and you didn't need me. Now *I* want to help *you* as much as I can. Let me start with Fred Bugsby."

Stonewall set his tea down. "Fred was an adult when I was born, so I didn't know him very well. However, he was into his eighties before passing on, so it's not difficult to put myself in his shoes." A pause. "Think about it. What was he like?"

"A miser?" I offered.

"Very rich," Lisa said.

"I'd say that sums him up. An old rich miser wouldn't be very popular, right? He'd look back—as I often do—and wonder what his life had meant and probably decide that in the face of death, money wasn't as important as he once thought."

Lisa volunteered another guess. "If he was afraid of dying, and wanted to be remembered even though nobody loved him . . . "

I snapped my fingers. "He could have set up a trust fund. Like the ones that give college scholarships."

"Except," Stonewall said, "he loved money and couldn't bear to give it away. Maybe a legend of his lost gold would be the perfect thing to leave behind. Nobody would ever forget him and the money would remain his, maybe forever. Are you with me so far?"

"Sure," I said. "But you could have guessed all of this before today. Why are you *now* suddenly so sure the treasure exists, when before you weren't."

"Ho, ho," Stonewall said gleefully. "I'm glad you listen so closely. What do I know now that I didn't know before you stopped by this afternoon."

"The contents of the trunk," Lisa said with hesitation.

"The contents of the trunk. Exactly. Old-fashioned pharmaceutical equipment. Equipment that might have been used in a laboratory sixty years ago."

We waited.

"I'm putting myself back in Fred's shoes again," Stonewall said. "I've got to leave my gold somewhere. After all, 1 can't just throw it away. Starting a legend appeals to me. Leaving a map in a book is the first clue. That map, once figured out, leads to another map. The second map leads to the trunk."

"Hah!" It hit me. "Everybody has assumed the trunk was the end of the line! It can be just another clue!"

"Yes," Stonewall said with satisfaction. "Another clue. Except an extremely difficult one."

"I'll say," I muttered.

"And here's where I gladly pay you back for returning to paint my sign. I'll tell you a story I once heard from my older brother many, many years ago. It might involve a laboratory, something that until this day I thought my brother was making up."

Stonewall tilted his head, as if listening to voices of the past. "My brother was your age when it happened, which meant it took place a year or two before I was born.

"Jamesville is a small town now. You can imagine in 1915 or 1916 that it was much smaller. Any stranger would be noticed instantly. Well, my brother happened to be near the train station making a delivery for my father during a snowstorm. Because of the storm, there were very few people around, so he was the only one to notice a tall fellow with a walrus moustache get off a train. The stranger part, of course, is only important to the story because he's the reason it begins. My brother trudged through the snow to ask if the stranger needed directions. Before he could get there, Fred Bugsby arrived and took the stranger by the arm.

"Normally, that might not be unusual. Fred was just starting his businesses then, and often had sales people stop by. My brother overheard the stranger's accent, however. It was British. So my brother, a great fan of Sherlock Holmes, decided to follow. It was easy of course, because the snow left tracks. The strange part was, the tracks ended at a new warehouse. My brother looked inside through a window and saw nobody. Yet there were no return footprints to show someone had left."

Stonewall stopped to take a deep breath. "By itself that strange bit of trivia might mean nothing. Except that happened to be the same warehouse which received many deliveries my brother made later throughout the next year. The packages, my brother told me, always contained pharmaceutical equipment. He put two and two together and came up with an explanation that I never did believe. Until today. You see, my brother was convinced Fred Bugsby had a secret laboratory there."

"A secret laboratory?" I scoffed. "That's only in movies."

"Exactly what I thought then," Stonewall said. "But . . . "

He reemphasized his last word. *"But* . . . consider if my brother's guess was true. Then the equipment in that trunk is a very big pointer to the next place to look for his gold."

"Great," I said. "Now we're looking for a legendary treasure in a secret laboratory in a building that's so old it may or may not exist. Do you want to throw in anything else to make this more realistic? Frankenstein's monster, perhaps?"

Lisa giggled. "In other words, Mr. Sawyer, we both know exactly how Ricky and Mike and Ralphy will be spending all of next Saturday. Searching again."

I sighed. Because, as usual, she was right.

It looked like a brown grape. An innocent brown grape on the far edge of a bag of fertilizer. Then, as I began to lift the bag and my arm brushed against it, a bunch of legs shot out from the grape and propelled it up my sleeve.

"Whaaahhhhh!" I spun and threw the bag over my head and backward. I followed that with a banshee dance that sent the spider higher inside my shirt and mashed my big toe against the stack of bags.

Twice. "Whhooooooh! Whhooooooh!"

The noise sent it deeper. Desperate, I tore off my shirt. That was a mistake because then I saw the spider in the middle of my chest and with legs in sight it suddenly seemed as large as a tomato. "Whaaahhhhh!" I hopped sideways and in panic flicked it free from my skin and across the dirt floor.

My heart decided it wasn't a rocket anymore, so I took a deep breath and bent forward to retrieve my shirt.

"That *HIC* was a nice try," Ralphy said after a moment. "No warning at all. Any louder and I think it would have scared me into *HIC* stopping for sure."

Mike remained uncharacteristically silent. I straightened and turned. He lay sprawled on the floor with the bag of fertilizer across his stomach. Only his eyes moved, and they beamed on me with full glare.

"It was a spider," I protested. "A big hairy one. It crawled up my shirt and I dropped the bag and ... "

"If that was a drop," Mike groaned, "remind me to take out insurance on your next throw." He pushed the bag away and slowly rolled to his feet.

I looked at Mike, then at Ralphy. Dirt had smeared masks on both of them, and their grimy shirts showed circles of sweat. Fresh sweat.

"Not such a good idea, huh guys?" The answer showed on their faces.

It was Saturday afternoon and the three of us — no surprise — were searching an old warehouse for a secret laboratory. Barely longer than our school gymnasium, and only half as wide, its ceiling cross beams were low enough to reach by jumping. The only light came from dangling light bulbs, and around us were stacks and stacks of fertilizer bags.

Since morning, we had been moving each stack three feet sideways.

Mike groaned again and wiped his brow. "Good idea? Let's put it this way, pal. I now regret being smart enough to go through those old files."

At the time, it had verged on genius. After I had told them what Stonewall had told me about a secret laboratory, Mike had remembered his floor scrubbing work in City Hall. "Land titles going back years," he had told us with a grin, "files and files worth. Wouldn't it make sense to find out what warehouses Moth-Wallet Bugsby once owned," Mike had asked us without dimming his grin, "then see which ones are still standing?"

In other words, he had bought Stonewall's story without a moment's hesitation.

The part of tracing down the one warehouse was simple.

Getting permission to go inside had also been simple. Mr. Schulz, who also owned the lumber and home improvement store next door, had simply shaken his head. "Crazy kids," he had said with a chuckle. "It's nothing but land with a roof overtop. Three people aside from me have owned it since Bugsby sold it and nothing of value has been found. Go ahead and waste your time. Anything you come up with is all yours. But have fun."

We had figured out his sarcastic grin as soon as we had walked in four hours earlier. Wrestling porcupines would have been more fun.

Dirt floors. Rough wood walls. And storage for bags of fertilizer, bags of grass seed, and bags of peat moss. Which had been agony to unstack and restack as we prodded the dirt floor with an iron rod.

I tried to be philosophical. "We've checked beneath three quarters of the stacks so far. You never know which of the next ones are covering the door to a fortune in gold."

Mike wiped his brow again. "Face it. We don't even know if this is the *right* warehouse."

"Fifty percent chance it is," Ralphy interrupted. "Simple mathematical chances. Those records showed that back in 1915, Moth-Wallet only owned two warehouses. One divided by two is 50 percent. Actually, the odds are even better considering that—"

"—that the other warehouse was torn down and no one discovered a secret laboratory," Mike finished wearily. "Come on, guys. We're moving tons of fertilizer sixty pounds at a time. Why? Because of a half-remembered story that was only some kid's guess back in 1915. I'll bet the rest of these stacks only cover more dirt. And I'll bet if anyone finds out how stupid we were, they'll laugh themselves to death."

"Don't beat around the bush," I commented. "You don't like our chances?"

"Hah, hah." Mike kicked an empty cardboard box in my direction.

The flap opened and showed another empty box inside. Both rattled as I kicked them back at Mike.

He brought his foot back to reboot them, and frowned in concentration. "Field goal attempt. Three points."

"Wait!" Ralphy blurted.

"Huh?" Mike lowered his foot.

Ralphy walked over to the empty boxes and stared down.

He thought so long that two more hiccups popped free from his stomach.

Then he looked up at both of us and grinned. "Got it."

Before we could comment on his obvious craziness, he dashed to the rickety doors at the front of the warehouse. Then he dashed towards us down the corridor formed by stacks of bags. Mike and I pressed back and Ralphy breezed by, counting aloud.

He reached the far wall, spun around, then sprinted by us again and out the warehouse doors.

Mike looked at me. I looked at him. "Private hiccup cure?"

Mike shrugged. "Another fake spider attack?"

"Hey! It wasn't fake. You would have jumped even farther if—"

Ralphy burst back inside the warehouse.

Even in the dim light, triumph showed clearly on his face.

He stopped in front of us, panting and hiccuping for a minute before getting his voice.

"The boxes," he said. "Come here and look at the boxes."

We did.

Ralphy squatted and pulled the smaller box out of the bigger one. "OK. Let this box be the *inside* of the warehouse." He dropped it back into the larger box.

"Sure," Mike said, looking down. "Except, I don't see three idiots moving fertilizer."

I waved him quiet as I suddenly understood.

"Mike," I said quietly, "now pretend the big box is the outside of the warehouse. Check out the space between the two of them."

He stared at it briefly, then brought his head up and nodded thoughtfully. "That's what Ralphy was doing. Measuring the length of the inside of the warehouse. Then the outside."

"Yup." Ralphy's eyes gleamed. "Twenty running steps front-to-back on the inside. Twenty-two steps front-to-back on the outside. With no hall at the front. *The lab isn't below us, it's sandwiched between the walls at the back of the warehouse!*"

He was right. It took less than five minutes of tapping across the rear wall for us to find a hollow section.

"Nuts," Mike said as a deeper knocking sound echoed back at the rap of the iron bar. "Four hours of killer work. Wasted."

Ralphy giggled. "Maybe it'll help you grow muscles."

Mike made a fist, but I grabbed it. "Later, guys. Look at that piece of wood."

It ran horizontally across the section of wall in front of us, a thin strip of rough lumber similar to the ones crossing all the other panels.

Ralphy noticed first. "Near the right side, it's worn a little smoother than the rest."

I nodded. "As if . . . " I grunted as I reached up to pull. ". . . someone's hand had grabbed it there many, many—"

It was that simple.

The wooden slat clicked downward under the pressure of my hand, and a panel the size of a door swung inward.

I sucked my breath in excitement.

The three of us stared in amazement.

"There really was a lab," Mike said. "I can't believe it."

"Me neither," I whispered. "It was just fun to dream about the legend being true. And now . . . "

Ralphy merely hiccuped, pulled the flashlight out from the back of his pants, flicked it on, and took a step forward into the secret space. Then he stepped back, and turned his suddenly white face to us.

"Skeletons?" Mike asked.

He shook his head and moved slowly to shine the flashlight on his arm at a bigger version of the spider that had attacked me. "Worse," he croaked. "Cobwebs."

The spider dropped to the floor and disappeared under a crack in the wall.

All of us retreated to our jackets and draped them over our heads and shoulders. We stepped through decades' worth of spider webs, shook our jackets clean, and finally we were there. In the center of a small chemistry lab that had been unvisited since the death of Moth-Wallet Bugsby.

"Wow," Mike said. "We should have no problem finding the gold in this small area."

I nodded agreement. The work area was barely double the width of the table that lined its entire length. To conserve space, shelves had been built into the back wall above and below the table. Each shelf was lined with rows and rows of the same old-fashioned crockery that had been found in the trunk.

The long table — a work bench — had copper tubing, test tubes, and more of the clay, enamel, and pewter beakers, crucibles, and crockery. All of the pieces were lined up in orderly rows.

Ralphy toned down his excitement and warned us. "Old Lady Bugsby's going to try to take this from us too."

I shook my head. "It won't be as easy as the first time. Stonewall already explained that to me. For starts, the warehouse isn't hers. Mr. Schulz might want some, but I'll bet he gives us a hefty reward. And, as Stonewall says, possession is nine-tenths of the law."

Ralphy grinned. "Just wanted to hear that again. Now that we're so close and all that."

Mike ignored us. He was already in motion, lifting some of the old boxes stored underneath the bench, moving others that were stacked beside the wall.

Without speaking more, Ralphy and I helped him search.

Two hours later we still had nothing.

There were boxes and boxes of old scrap paper. Invoices, bills, business letters filled with scraps of doodling and writing made it obvious Moth-Wallet Bugsby had been so cheap that he didn't like throwing out paper unless both sides had been used.

There were more instruments and weigh scales and empty beakers and pewter containers with chemicals. There were scrapbooks with newspaper clippings about Moth-Wallet's businesses. And there were enough spiders to fill a hundred nightmares.

But no gold.

We poked and prodded dirt, and tapped and knocked on walls, and searched the entire secret laboratory five times through and did not find a single thing which hinted at gold.

"Nothing," Mike finally said with sad resignation. "No gold. No map to another spot. I'm going to walk home and never think about it again. And you know why? Because we have looked so carefully that I know there's no chance we missed finding the gold in here. So I'm going home and calling this the end."

He shook his head at us. "Good night," he said quietly and walked away.

Ralphy said the same and followed him.

The worst part was that I knew with equal certainty that they were right. Moth-Wallet Bugsby's practical joke had just snagged three more victims.

I closed the door softly behind me and hurried to catch up to Mike and Ralphy.

In the darkness that had begun to fill the end of the afternoon, I told myself that Stonewall and his blues music were right about something else too.

Dreams do fall hard.

20

Studying the shadows on my bedroom ceiling had become a Saturday night habit. All because of Moth-Wallet Bugsby.

What seemed like a lifetime ago, I had lain awake most of a Saturday night worrying about the punishment for shooting a watermelon into Moth-Wallet's statue.

The following Saturday, I had been unable to sleep because of the excitement of finding his map. The Saturday after that, depression caused by Ethel Bugsby's book buying had kept me awake.

This Saturday night was no different. Except for one thing. I couldn't understand what was keeping me awake.

I ran the day's events through my mind. Sure, we had found the secret laboratory. But no gold, and no clues to its location. Ralphy, Mike, and I were through with dreaming about the treasure. We certainly weren't going to let anyone else know about the laboratory, but we were positive there was no gold. So wondering what to do with a new fortune wasn't the reason I was halfway through memorizing the shadows above my bed.

Then I ran through a checklist of other things which might keep me awake. I ticked them off. No, I didn't have any overdue library books. No, I didn't have a test on Monday. No, I wasn't failing any subjects. No, report cards weren't due for a while anyway. No, Mike hadn't done anything new which might get us in trouble.

I sighed. I had a reasonably clear conscience, so *that* wasn't the reason I watched the minutes pass by on my digital radio clock.

Then I replayed our search of the laboratory in my mind. Yes, we had searched every box and scanned every piece of paper. Yes, we had made sure every inch of the dirt floor was actually dirt. Yes, we had checked above the cross beams of the open ceiling. Yes, we had looked underneath the table top. Yes, we had gone through every shelf five times. So *that* couldn't be bugging me.

I stopped breathing for a couple of heartbeats.

I replayed everything again. *What had been unusual just enough to nag me now?*

In the dark, I shook my head in frustration. Nothing.

Then, slowly, it eased into my memory. A large crockery pot with bits of curled and charred paper. I had turned it over to empty the burnt pieces and found nothing.

I shook my head again. That couldn't be it.

I thought about other things. Lisa's smile. Stonewall's saxophone. Ralphy hiccupping. Joel always disappearing.

It didn't work. My mind kept returning to the charred paper.

I tried picturing the container as I had picked it up.

At the top had been the corner of an envelope. Flames had once licked the edges of course, but half of a return address had been plain. Two words stuck in my mind. *Kendall. London.*

I clenched my fists and fought back from screaming in frustration. *What was so different about the burned paper that wouldn't let me sleep?*

Then, as my fingers unclenched, it dawned on me.

Cheap old Moth-Wallet Bugsby had saved boxes and boxes of

scrap paper. Why would he go to the trouble of burning some? Unless he had something to hide. And that something to hide would have been that letter. And my only clues to its contents were *Kendall* and *London.*

It took me an hour.

I actually sat up in bed and stared out my window at the glow of the streetlight and lost myself in concentration for an hour. Little things over the last four weeks — bits of conversations with Stonewall and other grown-ups, scraps of information from the history books, land titles in the city hall basement, and even clues from the first map — finally added up.

When the hour was finished, I believed I knew it would take only five minutes in the library on Monday to confirm that the sum of my addition meant a treasure in gold. It didn't give me as much satisfaction as I expected. Because when the hour was finished, I also knew too much more about the ugliness of a mean-spirited man who had been filled with greed his entire life.

I spent another hour in equally deep concentration fighting to think through a plan that might remedy a tiny part of that greed.

And finally I slept.

21

"Trust me," I said to Mike's questioning look.

He shook his head as he took a break from loading boxes in the dim light of Moth-Wallet Bugsby's secret laboratory. "My mother told me to never," he repeated, "*never* trust anyone who says 'trust me.'"

I snorted. "Just keep loading."

He frowned at me in suspicion. "My mother also told me never to trust anyone with dirty fingernails."

"Trust me anyway."

"And where did you disappear to at noon today, anyhow? Mondays we always play volleyball during the lunch break."

I shrugged. "Just keep loading."

He grumbled under his breath. "Why can't Lisa and Ralphy be here to help?"

I smiled. "The fewer the better on this. Trust me."

I hid my worries from him. Because it was less trust, and more a thing of fear on my part. The near certainty of Saturday night's theory had vanished. I was no longer sure of the truth. Worse, I was scared to discover I might be right, and more scared to discover I might be wrong. And if my plan failed . . . well, it would be better to take the blame all by myself.

So once again, I smiled away my worries. "Trust me, pal. Keep loading these boxes and tomorrow after school I'll deliver them to Old Lady Bugsby."

* * * * * * * *

The bong of an ancient doorbell echoed throughout Old Lady Bugsby's house

She answered immediately. Which didn't surprise me. I had seen a window curtain move as I hauled Joel's wagon up the wide sidewalk leading to her front porch.

"Yes," she snapped.

I wondered if her entire wardrobe consisted of black dresses. Except, of course, for the one that was dark purple from ink. I fought the urge to smirk as I noticed that her hair was shaded funny and her hands were still stained from the grand trunk opening.

"We found more of your father's stuff," I replied.

She glared at me. "Obviously it's not the gold. Otherwise you wouldn't be bringing it here."

Under her withering gaze, I began to stare at my feet and began to shuffle nervously.

"Well . . . "

"Spit it out."

"It's . . . um . . . more of the same stuff that was in the trunk." I corrected myself hastily and glanced up. "But I don't mean ink. That crockery stuff. Me and my friends found it in an old warehouse."

She stiffened suddenly. I thought I heard her say the word *impossible* under her breath.

I quickly looked down again.

She recovered by lashing out at me.

"You mean 'my friends and I.' And look at me when I'm speaking to you."

I forced my head up. Her eyes glittered black.

The tone of her voice harshened. "Tell me. Did you find any gold that you've decided to keep a secret?"

I shook my head.

"Then I'm not interested in having you bother me with junk."

"I just thought . . . " I faltered under the scorch of her eyes.

"You just thought what," she spat out.

"This stuff does belong to you and I didn't want to get in trouble for keeping it and then I thought . . . "

"Yes, yes," she said. "Quit mumbling."

"Well, I thought you might want to pay me to sell it for you. As a reward or something."

"A reward?" Her voice nearly became a screech. "Reward for cluttering my place with junk?"

I stepped back with uncertainty. "This stuff might bring forty or fifty bucks or even more. You never know with garage sales. And if you gave me a 20 percent commission . . . "

She stepped forward to glare down her nose at me. "Twenty percent! I can sell it myself."

I winced. "Yes ma'am. But I'd let people on my paper route know. And I'd set the table up outside and stand there for as long as it took to sell."

She merely continued glaring at me.

"Fifteen percent?" I offered.

"Ten percent," she snapped. "And I'll be around to make sure you don't steal the profits."

"Yes ma'am." I paused. "On Saturday? When I'm out of school?"

She nodded.

"Should I leave these boxes here?" I asked.

She shook her head with mild disgust. "Of course not. Take that clutter home until Saturday. You think I'm paying you good money to do absolutely nothing?"

22

Saturday, I thought as I stood behind a table set up in front of Old Lady Bugsby's house, *again*. Five Saturdays had passed since all of this began with the destruction of her father's statue.

The sidewalk in front of me was empty in both directions as far as I could see. *What if nobody showed up as promised? My plan would fail before it even began.*

It gave me time to think. Grown-ups are lucky. Their lives aren't restricted to being lived on Saturdays. But us kids, that's a different matter. School days on one side, Sundays with all the after-church family visits that drive a guy nuts on the other side. Only Saturdays give us the freedom to do what we want.

So what was I doing stuck with a table full of ancient crockery in front of the house owned by the meanest lady in Jamesville?

Wishing this Saturday would end, that's what. Even if the sun was shining early enough to make this fall day pleasantly warm.

"Not much of an idea, was it?"

I jumped. She was as bad as Joel for sneaking up on people.

"That's right," Old Lady Bugsby continued. "I'll be checking on you all day." She stopped long enough to snort scorn. "Not that it looks like you'll have much to steal from me if you keep selling at this rate."

Mrs. Reynolds, in a flowered dress, walked around the corner of the block.

Rescued!

"Hello, Ricky," she called. "Hello, Ethel. Fine day, isn't it."

"Hmmph," Old Lady Bugsby muttered to me. "Mind you give back the correct change."

Before I could reply, she clicked her high heels in retreat.

Mrs. Reynolds stopped in front of the table. "Obviously Ethel hasn't forgiven me for letting her buy her books back at double the price."

I shrugged, not sure whether I was allowed to agree with her conclusion about another grown-up.

Mrs. Reynolds looked at the crockery. "I'll buy three," she said.

"That'll be fifteen dollars, ma'am," I said.

Before she could say anything, I glanced over her shoulder.

"And here comes Mr. Schulz and Mayor Thorpe," I announced.

I plucked the bills from her hand, quickly placed the change in her palm, and put the crockery into one of the grocery bags I had stacked on the table.

I faced the new customers.

"Hello, sirs," I said.

Mr. Schulz spoke first. "So this is the junk you found in my warehouse." He nudged Mayor Thorpe. "The kid's quite a salesman to get me to buy two of them back."

"It's for a good cause," I protested. "The profits from this sale will go to feeding people in third world countries."

Mayor Thorpe chuckled. "You told me it was for a local church project."

"That too," I said quickly. I smiled lamely. "The profits are going to be divided, that's all."

Mayor Thorpe exchanged looks with Mr. Schulz and rolled his eyeballs. "Sure. Sure. Just give me the two I agreed to order."

"Ten dollars each, gentlemen."

Then everybody arrived at once. Mike's mom. Ralphy's dad. My mom. Lisa's dad. Lisa. Mike. Ralphy. Even Pastor Stan from our church. All of them bought two each.

Mike leaned forward and grumbled above the noise of everybody chatting. "I don't see why I'm giving you ten bucks for stuff *we* found. Especially since it's going to Old Lady Bugsby." He caught the grin in my eyes. "I know. I know. Trust you."

He shook his head and handed me two fives.

Lisa, who had been chatting with Mayor Thorpe, returned to the table.

"Most of the stuff's been sold. Can you leave now?"

"Not by a long shot!" came a voice from behind me. "There's still a mess to be cleaned up."

I jumped again and when I landed, I shook my head no in apology to Lisa.

When everybody left, Old Lady Bugsby came around to the front of the table. "You've sold twenty-three. That should mean a hundred and fifteen dollars. Let's see it."

I handed over the sheaf of bills.

She counted through slowly. Twice. Then nodded grudgingly as her eyes scanned the near empty table. "Seven left. I expect to find another forty dollars when you're through."

"Yes ma'am. And my commission?"

"You'll get it later. Although why I ever agreed to 10 percent is beyond me. Five percent would be plenty."

She spun on her heel and left me alone at the table.

Seven pieces left.

I waited.

Finally, I saw my last two customers.

Stonewall Sawyer moved slowly up the sidewalk, guided by the leather harness attached to Blue, and holding Joel's hand in the other.

"Beautiful day, isn't it?" Stonewall said when he reached the edge of the table. To confirm it, he lifted his face to the sun and felt the warmth.

"Yes, sir."

He fumbled in his pockets for his wallet. Blue sat down and began to wait patiently. Joel squatted beside Blue and scratched his muzzle.

"Stonewall!" For the third time that morning, I jumped. Maybe Old Lady Bugsby and Joel should start a club, I thought sourly.

"Ethel Bugsby," Stonewall said stiffly. "It's been a long time."

"Yes," she sniffed. "A town this small, you'd figure old people like us would run into each other more often."

It was hard to tell whether she thought that was good or bad.

"Being on different sides of the tracks has a habit of doing that to people," Stonewall said. "Remember? My brother was the one who weeded your father's garden for five cents an hour."

Old Lady Bugsby's face grew mean. "Still carrying a grudge. Fine. Ricky, charge him double."

Before I could say anything, Stonewall shushed me. "It's not worth it, son. I promised I'd help out your sale, and I won't change my mind." He handed me twenty dollars.

"Five left," Ethel crowed. "And already a hundred sixty!"

"One left, ma'am," I corrected her. "My brother Joel busted into his piggy bank to buy two of them, and I'm buying two."

I nodded at Joel. He stopped scratching Blue long enough to pull ten crumpled dollar bills from his pocket.

"We'll be leaving now," Stonewall said with dignity. "You're welcome to stop by later for tea, son. I believe there's still a few old tunes you haven't heard yet."

Joel gave me a questioning look and I nodded again, so he struggled with the bags, including one with my two smaller pieces, and followed Stonewall's slow progress away from us.

"Well," Old Lady Bugsby said. "So it is. One left. I expect you to be here until it's sold."

"Yes, ma'am. I hope you'll take the ten dollars I owe you out of my commission."

Her brows furrowed. "Just don't expect commission on the ones you sold to yourself."

I sighed. "Yes, ma'am."

As she turned to retreat to her house, I accidentally bumped the table.

The remaining piece tottered on the edge, and I overreacted. As I made a wild grab for it, I swept it off the table. It flew five feet and shattered in front of Old Lady Bugsby's feet.

"You clumsy fool!" she screeched. "I'm deducting this from your com—"

She stopped herself in midsentence.

Her voice sounded strangled when—without turning to face me—she started speaking again. "Run to the house, Ricky. Get a broom to clean up this mess."

I hesitated. *Was it my imagination, or was there a small folded piece of paper among the shards in front of her on the sidewalk?*

"Now!" she ordered. "Don't waste my time."

When I returned, she stood beside the table, tapping her foot with impatience.

"Sale's over," she announced. "I've decided to keep this last one for myself."

I looked at her, then began to sweep.

"That's enough for today," she said. She reached into her pocket and handed me some bills without counting. "Take these and go. I'll handle the rest of this."

A secret smile played across her face.

Before I reached the corner down the block, I took a final look.

Maybe I was too far away, but I thought I saw her pull something white from a pocket of her black dress.

Fifteen minutes after leaving Old Lady Bugsby, I was anxious to find out if I truly did have a reason for selling all that crockery except the last piece.

That meant I needed to find Mike or Ralphy or Lisa.

Naturally, when I was busting inside from curiosity, they were nowhere to be found. Not at any of their homes, not at the schoolyard, not anywhere.

All right, I told myself, *the next best thing is to find Joel.* No luck there, either.

By that time, I'd wasted an hour.

So I told myself I would finally test out my theory at Stonewall's house. I didn't want to spend long there, but I knew testing the theory would take less than a minute, and since he was blind, he wouldn't notice what I was doing. That way, if I'd been wrong, at least he wouldn't be disappointed.

Music, of course, reached me from his front porch as I approached the house.

Then voices. I mentally kicked myself. *That's* where everybody was today.

"He's been acting weird all week," I heard Mike say. "All I heard was 'trust me,' 'trust me.'"

"He must have had a good reason for this," Lisa said. "He knows we aren't made of money."

We'll see about that, I told myself.

Blue barked a greeting as I moved into the doorway. Ralphy hiccupped his.

"Did someone say the word *weird?*" I asked cheerfully.

Mike blushed.

"Well . . . "

"I'll let you know why I had to get rid of all the crockery," I began as I moved inside. "But first promise to keep this a secret. You'll understand when I explain."

I waited until everyone nodded, including Stonewall, who had an amused smile on his face.

I took a deep breath. "The most important thing I needed to do was prevent Old Lady Bugsby from—"

Blue growled.

I darted to the window.

Old Lady Bugsby was entering the yard through the gate. Behind her, pushing and shoving, followed Yellow Fingers and Squinty Eyes.

"Nuts," I hissed. "We need to hide! Everyone except Stonewall!"

They stared at me as if I were crazy.

"Come on!" I pleaded. "You've gone with me this far. Just listen this last time."

They might not have moved if Stonewall hadn't spoken quietly. "You may all go into my bedroom. You should be safe there."

He pointed in the direction of a door down the short hallway.

I ran quickly, hoping the others would follow.

They did, and I shut the door, but I still couldn't relax.

"Ralphy, grab a pillow. If you feel a hiccup coming, muffle it."

Doubt filled his face, but he grabbed one anyway.

"What is this?" Lisa whispered.

"Shhhh!"

We all heard the clumping of footsteps as Old Lady Bugsby and her escorts reached the front porch.

"Stonewall! Stonewall Sawyer!" Her voice reached us as clearly as Blue's menacing growl.

"Yes."

"How can I come in with that dog blocking the door? Would you ask him to leave?"

Silence.

Then Stonewall's voice. "Blue, into the kitchen."

His bedroom wall was so thin, we could even hear the padding of Blue's feet.

"Shut the door behind him," came Old Lady Bugsby's commanding voice.

The steady footsteps of Squinty Eyes or Yellow Fingers and the click of the door followed. Then footsteps back.

"That's better," she said. "May I sit?"

"I'd rather you didn't."

More silence.

"Stonewall," she finally said. "I've come to make amends."

"Amends." His voice had none of its regular warmth.

"I've been thinking about what you said earlier. How your brother gardened for my father at five cents an hour."

Even from our hidden position, we could hear ice in Stonewall's voice. "Our family needed even that meager bit of income to survive. And you know the reason behind that. How do you expect to make amends seventy years later?"

"Stonewall, Stonewall," she crooned. "Don't get stiff-necked with pride. You had the misfortune of making it big when musicians didn't get paid the way they do today. We both know you don't have a lot of money."

"Blue and I do just fine."

"In a one-bedroom house?"

"We do fine."

Silence again. I could imagine Old Lady Bugsby's fierce eyes measuring Stonewall.

"I won't beat around the bush," she said. "You're not a charity case, but I want you to have money. It's my way of trying to make up. I'll offer you double what this house is worth."

"Double," Stonewall stated without agreeing.

"That should let you move somewhere more comfortable."

A pause before Stonewall spoke. "I don't think so. This is the house my father bought when your father forced him out of business. It has sentimental value."

"That's exactly it!" Old Lady Bugsby exclaimed. "What better way could there be to make amends? You getting all that money for something my father forced your father to buy?"

Stonewall's sigh was loud. "I still don't think so."

Beside me, Ralphy hiccupped into the pillow. My shoulders slumped in relief at how little noise it made.

Old Lady Bugsby's voice grew edgy. "Stonewall, don't be a stubborn fool. I'll give you triple what it's worth."

Stonewall coughed. "Triple? But I am *very—*" He stressed it again. "*—very* attached to it. Sentimental reasons and all that."

Old Lady Bugsby laughed. "I can tell you're interested. Triple is my final offer. But if you *are* so sentimental, I'll let you rent it back from me."

Stonewall said firmly, "Add ten thousand to the price, and it's yours. I'll move out."

"Then no rental and move out by Monday," Old Lady Bugsby countered. "I've got the check here."

"I'm blind."

"My two friends here will help you move."

Stonewall let out a long breath. "I meant I can't read the check."

"Come, come, Stonewall. You can trust me."

"Like my father trusted your father?"

A very long silence. Then from Old Lady Bugsby, "I'm writing and signing the check, Stonewall. Do you want it or not?"

Suddenly, Stonewall raised his voice. "Lisa! If you're finished in the bedroom, please come out here."

His voice dropped. "She cleans house for me on Saturdays."

Old Lady Bugsby hissed, "You could have told me."

"Would it have made a difference?" he asked as Lisa moved to the bedroom door.

Her reply was lost as Lisa closed the door behind her.

Stonewall asked Lisa, "What does the check read?"

Lisa told him.

"Fine," Stonewall said. "Now I'm sure Miss Bugsby has something she wants me to sign."

We next heard a rustling of papers and a grunt of approval from Old Lady Bugsby.

Her next words startled all of us. "Hah! Hah! I've got the house now! Stonewall, you fool. Do you think I really wanted to make amends?"

He said nothing to that question, only raised his voice to us in the bedroom. "The rest of you can come out now. Because I want some answers."

We filed out.

"This is unusual," Old Lady Bugsby said through a tight frown. "But it doesn't change anything. The house is mine."

"As you say," Stonewall said. Some of the warmth had edged back into his voice. "But I'd like Ricky to explain something."

"What's that," she snapped. "I've haven't all day."

Stonewall first held the check out in front of him. "Please keep this for me, Lisa," he said.

He waited until she had done so.

"Ricky," Stonewall then asked, "why did you tell me yesterday that I could expect Miss Bugsby to make me an offer on my house? And why did you insist I force the price high?"

Was I ready to explain? It's one thing to think you know everything when alone in the comforting darkness late at night in your bedroom. It's another to explain it in the light of day.

Then I realized something. If I was wrong, I couldn't be in worse trouble than I already was. So I plunged in.

"Miss Bugsby, did James Kendall know what your father intended to do with his discovery?"

She sucked in a breath so quickly it almost became a whistle. Then she recovered. "James Kendall," she said coolly. "I don't believe that's a familiar name."

What evidence did I have? Secondhand information about a long ago and barely remembered visit with a British stranger, the scraps of a burnt envelope, a hidden laboratory, and some encyclopedia facts. If she didn't admit to anything, two hundred years of good behavior wouldn't get me out of the mess caused by a con job that might have worked all too well.

"He wrote one of your father's twelve books which you purchased back from the library. *A Thesis on Laboratory Techniques* by James Kendall."

Yellow Fingers and Squinty Eyes stared at me blankly. But Old Lady Bugsby's eyes had narrowed with malice.

"And what of it?" she said.

"Well," I said as slowly as possible, "James Kendall corresponded with your father."

"You have no proof of that!"

"Yes, ma'am," I apologized. "Actually, I do." Not that I wanted her to know it was simply a corner of an envelope decades old. "We found it along with the crockery and other laboratory stuff." I paused. "Laboratory stuff that could easily duplicate James Kendall's discovery."

"Not possible." Her voice had become a croak.

At that, I sensed, sadly, that the knowledge about her father had been her private misery for many years.

"I can tell Stonewall if you don't care to," I said.

Her head straightened and her face regained its cunning sharpness. "Stonewall doesn't know?"

I shook my head. "Not yet."

"Your friends don't know?"

I shook my head. "I was about to tell them—"

A look appeared in her eyes that I had never seen before in anyone's eyes. It was as if a light had been shut off, to be replaced by a dark and insane fury.

She reached into her purse. "Good," she said with detached calm. "They won't get a chance to know either."

When she pulled free from her purse, her knuckles were such a tight white that her hand was barely more than a claw gripping the tiny gun pointed in my direction.

"Not another word," she said in a harsh whisper. "Don't think I won't use this." She cackled. "My little friend here has been with me for years. You can never trust who might rob you. And now my little friend will help keep my father's name clear."

Stonewall spoke calmly. "Ethel. You don't sound well. Whatever you're doing, it's not worth it. Your father's dead."

Her laugh was hideous. "Every night I talk to my father. I

know he listens. I know he wants me to do this."

Behind her, Yellow Fingers and Squinty Eyes watched in the same frozen horror that held all of us.

The hideous noises from her mouth continued. "My father was a saint. He even made sure I would have money in my old age by turning it into gold and hiding it for me."

She glared at us and sobered with insane quickness. "It's not his fault, I let him down. It's not his fault I was too dumb to find it. But today! I know where it is, and I'll tell my father tonight that I was a good girl. I'll tell him I've got it all."

"Ethel," Stonewall began in soothing tones.

"Shut up!" She pulled the hammer of the gun back and lifted the barrel so that it was facing my chest.

"Nobody will hear this boy tell lies about my father!"

That's when Joel moved to stand in front of me.

"I won't let you hurt my brother," he said stoutly.

It would have been funny if I weren't so filled with terror. Some protection. His head barely reached my chest. *Joel, you dimwit,* a detached part of me thought.

As if in a dream, I stepped in front of Joel. The black hole of the wavering gun was only five feet away. "Please don't shoot him," I said. "He's too young."

Joel scrambled around to get in front of me again.

I pushed him aside. He grunted and pushed back.

Mike told me later that her gun didn't waver for a second. Mike told me later that she had just closed her eyes to pull the trigger.

I didn't see it.

My final shove had thrown Joel to the floor at Stonewall's feet, when a black blur knocked me face forward.

Then an explosion filled my ears and the sudden crash against my skull was a thunderclap of pain that put me into darkness.

25

At first, as I came out of the darkness, I thought the muffled sobs were mine.

I tried speaking before my eyes blinked open, and found out they couldn't belong to me—but my tongue was blocked and I sputtered instead.

More cool water on my face, and I discovered I was sitting against one of Stonewall Sawyer's stuffed chairs.

Lisa had a glass of water in one hand and a damp cloth in the other. Mike and Joel and Ralphy stared at me in wonder.

The muffled sobs continued somewhere beyond them.

Ralphy hiccupped a reassuring hello but my return smile didn't work. I spat something from my mouth. *A chunk of plaster?*

Mike explained softly. "Her shot hit the ceiling above you. Knocked some of it loose and it hit your head."

I blinked again. "The ceiling? How did she miss?"

Lisa shushed me. "While you and Joel distracted her, I opened the kitchen door. Blue knocked her down."

I finally looked past them, and understood the hush in their voices. Stonewall was at the far side of the room, his arm around Old Lady Bugsby's heaving shoulders. She was on her knees and each new sob convulsed her completely.

"The others?" I asked.

"They took off as soon as the gun fired," Mike said.

I began to ask something else, but Old Lady Bugsby's voice stopped me.

"Lord," she began. Her voice did not crack with the insane fury of a woman possessed. "You know how much I've done wrong. Please give me another chance and the grace to accept the punishment I deserve."

Another sob stopped her from continuing.

"Amen," Stonewall finished for her.

She buried her face on his shoulder.

Stonewall turned his face in our direction. "For now," he said, "let's not call in the police. Ethel has carried a big burden most of her life, and it appears the strain finally broke her. As you can see, it's unlikely she would do something like that again, and someone her age, well . . . "

I nodded, then corrected it to a quiet "yes" for Stonewall.

"Maybe we should go," Lisa suggested quietly. "We can leave Joel with Blue, but Stonewall and Miss Bugsby have probably got more things to talk about."

Mike poked me. "I know *Ricky* does."

I also knew why she had gone crazy. The big burden she had carried was her father's crime. Her family was gone, and so was Stonewall's. She was the only one left to pay for her father's crimes, and he was the only one left who had suffered because of them.

So when we filed out, Miss Ethel Bugsby no longer seemed to me a horrible witch. Instead, she was a tired, worn woman seeking comfort from the only person on earth who was able to give her the forgiveness she needed.

* * * * * * * *

"Wait until we get to the library," I said firmly. "Once you see what I found, I probably won't have to explain."

When we got there, Mrs. Reynolds simply shook her head at the plaster dust ground into my shoulders. I noted with satisfaction that her three pieces of crockery were on a shelf behind the checkout counter.

I marched straight to the encyclopedia section.

"K, k, k," I muttered as I thumbed through the books. "Here it is."

I pulled a volume free. "Kendall, Kendall, Kendall," licking my forefinger to flip the pages.

They crowded so close to me that I could feel their breathing on my neck.

"Here it is. James Kendall." It was fun keeping them in suspense. I began walking back to a table.

When they were seated, I read aloud a simple summary. "James Kendall. British scientist. Isolated the dysentery bacillus in 1915."

I let that hang there.

Ralphy was the first to speak. "Bacillus! That means the dysentery germ! *HIC*. The same thing that plagued the Sawyers!"

I read more. "Dysentery. A highly contagious disease spread through contamination, usually transmitted through impure water."

Lisa's eyes grew wide as she too realized the implications. "The perfect crime," she whispered with awe.

Mike looked from Ralphy to Lisa to me. "You're saying that Kendall is the strange British visitor who poisoned the Sawyers."

"Almost, pal," I said. "I *am* guessing the stranger was Kendall. It was well known that Moth-Wallet Bugsby was interested in science. I'm guessing they had a correspondence. Kendall was probably in the area anyway, or there by Bugsby's express invitation. I'm almost positive that much of what he wanted to learn from Kendall was how to isolate the dysentery germ."

"The perfect crime," Lisa repeated. "Who back then knew much about germs and contagious diseases? Moth-Wallet Bugsby could have found dozens of ways to slip contaminated water into the Sawyers' well. Nobody would dream it was being planted."

"But why?" Ralphy protested. He was rarely able to think badly of people.

"Think of it," I said. "You're so hungry for money that you don't mind if your biggest competitor is too sick to work anymore."

Mike slapped the table. "And every time the competitor gets better, you just recontaminate the water."

I nodded. "Stonewall was born blind because his mother was so ill. The entire family suffered."

"What will Stonewall say about that now?" Lisa wondered.

I pictured how we had left them. "I think Stonewall's prepared to forgive. Even if Moth-Wallet took advantage of the situation and went one step farther. Remember that Stonewall once mentioned how Ethel's father had lent his father some money?"

"Yup," Mike said.

"I went back and looked up more of those land titles. In 1919, every property and business that the Sawyers owned was taken in a foreclosure. Guess who foreclosed and guess who picked up the businesses and properties for next to nothing?"

"Not Santa Claus," Mike answered.

"Moth-Wallet Bugsby," I told them unnecessarily. "By making sure Stonewall's father stayed ill, he made sure the money couldn't be paid back. Then he repossessed. It was the start of his great fortune. And Ethel somehow knew it all along. That's why she went crazy today."

After several moments of silence, Mike snapped his fingers. "Hey! You still haven't told us why you knew Old Lady Bugsby would be buying Stonewall's house today."

I grinned. "That, my friends, is a whole new story."

Epilogue

●

I made them wait. Only ten minutes, but long enough for me to have a short—and private—talk with Mrs. Reynolds.

When I returned, Mike asked, "What was *she* yelling about. Doesn't she know the rules of her own library?"

I grinned again. "That too is a whole new story. Why don't I start with Old Lady Bugsby."

"Any *HIC* thing," Ralphy insisted quickly.

"Mike asked me on Monday where I had gone during the noon hour volleyball. In fact, he asked me just after pointing out how dirty my fingernails were."

"So?" Mike grunted.

"I had been working with clay in the art room. Enough clay to make one crucible."

Mike drummed his fingers on the table. "Get to it."

I whistled and stared at the ceiling.

"OK," he finally said through gritted teeth. "I apologize."

"In the clay of the crucible," I said sweetly, "I had planted a new map to Moth-Wallet's treasure of gold. A map that said it was hidden in Stonewall's house."

Lisa began laughing. "Let me guess. You set up the entire sale just to have that piece of crockery left over."

"Something like that. I dropped it and it broke at her feet. Her greediness made it too easy to fool her into believing it was an authentic map. She got me out of there so fast, she overpaid me for my work."

"That's terrible!" Ralphy exclaimed. "Tricking her into spending all that money."

I nodded. "Yup. But no one forced her to do it. And you have to admit there's not many other ways for Stonewall to get back some of his family's money after all this time has passed since the original crime."

"He'll give it back to her," Lisa predicted.

"Probably," I agreed.

"Fine, fine, fine," Mike said. "Why was Mrs. Reynolds yelling?"

Ralphy hiccupped loudly and winced. But no lectures came from the checkout desk. Which didn't surprise me.

"Tell me," I said. "Who all bought crockery at that sale this morning?"

Lisa listed them. "I guess you needed a lot of people to make it look like a real sale. All of our parents. Mayor Thorpe. Pastor Stan. Mr. Schulz. Mrs. Reynolds. You. Me. Ralphy. Mike."

"Joel and Stonewall," I finished for her. "All people who helped us, or, like Pastor Stan, who could put extra money to good use."

"Fine, fine, fine," Mike groaned. "Just quit talking in circles."

"Come on, Mike," I replied patiently. "What was the last saying on the original treasure map?"

He thought briefly. " 'Things beneath the surface of sight, provide a treasure to one who sees it right.' "

"Yup. Don't you think it strange that a miserly chemist would use all that bulky crockery for crucibles and beakers when glass would have been easier to use and much less expensive."

Lisa sat bolt upright as Ralphy hiccupped again. "Don't tell me!" she nearly shouted.

I smiled and nodded. "Gold covered by clay or enamel or pewter is definitely something beneath the surface of sight."

Mike's mouth dropped. Ralphy's face turned instantly white.

"You mean . . . " Mike began.

I smiled wider. ". . . I mean Mrs. Reynolds yelled because I just took a pair of scissors and scratched through the pewter of the crockery she bought this morning. She might have enough gold there to buy the convertible we promised her."

I shrugged modestly. "I also mean all of us bought that stuff fair and square from Old Lady Bugsby. She won't be able to use any kind of law to take it away from all of us."

I thought again and shook my head. "I'm sure, though, our parents will make us sock that money away for college or something else not fun."

Ralphy slumped forward and groaned.

He groaned steadily for three minutes.

The rest of us exchanged puzzled looks.

Ralphy finally sat up again. "I can't believe it," he moaned. "I just can't believe it."

"What?" Lisa asked.

"The stuff I bought from Ricky this morning. It's gone."

"No way," Mike said.

Ralphy groaned again. "My parents only went along with Ricky because I supplied them the money. I figured it was easier than trying to convince them to trust him."

"You mean you didn't trust me?" I asked with mock horror.

"Nooooo, I didn't." Real pain escaped him. "I just didn't want to argue with you."

"But all your gold?" Mike said quickly. "It can't be gone."

A single tear left the corner of Ralphy's eye. "I pitched it in the trash can just before meeting you guys at Stonewall's house this afternoon. And the garbagemen always come by on Saturdays."

Lisa put a gentle hand on his arm. "Ralphy, there's still enough daylight to ride your bike to the dump."

Ralphy's chin straightened with resolve. "That's right. There is. I'm going to search every piece of trash."

Without even saying good-bye, he dashed from the table.

"Should we help?" Lisa asked.

"Yuck," Mike said. "You know how smelly that job would be."

"Besides," I pointed out. "After the sale, I stopped by his house looking for you guys. When I cut through his backyard, I saw all the pieces sitting on top of a trash can, so I rescued all his gold. It's safe at my place."

Lisa giggled. "Why didn't you tell him?"

"He should have trusted me," I said. "But that's not the real reason."

They gave me strange looks.

"You'll notice he moaned and groaned for five minutes without interrupting himself once? The thought of losing all that gold scared the hiccups right out of him."

I blew on my fingernails and buffed them casually against my shoulder.

"He's a cured man," I finished as I leaned back in my chair and kicked my feet up. "Just call me Dr. Kidd."

How long could I have enjoyed that cool pose of triumph?

Probably hours. And the ten seconds I enjoyed were definitely not enough. When Joel tapped me on the shoulder, I did a backflip of terror that left me sprawled beneath an overturned chair and him clapping his hands in admiration.

Lisa looked over the edge of the table. "Need a *real* doctor?"

Joel stepped on two of my fingers running away from me.